Exposed

She never forgot the small town she came from, or the trouble she left behind...

Unfinished Business
Book 1

Juanita Kees

Exposed
Juanita Kees

She never forgot the small town she came from, or the trouble she left behind...

A woman entangled in a web of conflict, confronted by her tumultuous past. As Peta Johnson searches for her missing daughter in a race against the clock, she embarks on a journey of resilience and healing. But when threats lurk around every corner, can she trust the one man she's desperate to keep her secrets from?

Jaime Caruso left his heart in Williams when he decided to pursue a military career. Back in town to help his ailing father, Jaime wants nothing more than to pack up the family business and move it away from the memories. Until he comes face-to-face with his past.

Swept up in a nightmare that holds an innocent little girl captive, he's faced with choices he never wanted to make. Choices that lives depend on.

Contents

About the Author

Finding hope in country towns with dark secrets ...

Juanita escapes the real world to create emotionally engaging stories steeped in crime, suspense, mystery and intrigue. Her books are set in dusty, rural outback Australia and on the NASCAR racetracks of America. Her small-town USA and Australian rural stories have made the Amazon bestseller and top 100 lists. Juanita also likes to dabble in the ponds of fantasy and paranormal with Greek gods brought to life in the 21st century.

Juanita graduated college with distinctions and a diploma in Proofreading, Editing and Publishing in 2011 and started her freelance writing business, Kees2Create Words. As a developmental and structural editor, she assists writers to polish their manuscripts for submission. In 2012, she achieved her dream of becoming a published author and now has multiple novels on the market.

When she's not working, writing, editing or proofreading, Juanita enjoys travelling to discover new worlds for inspiration. Mother to two handsome heroes and partner to a car enthusiast, Juanita also has a passion for fast cars and country living.

Juanita loves to talk books with readers and would love to connect. Contact her via:

Amazon Author:
https://www.amazon.com/author/juanitakees
Website:
https://juanitakees.com/contact/
Kees2Create Words Editing:
https://kees2createwords.com/
Bookbub:
https://www.bookbub.com/authors/juanita-kees
Newsletter:
https://kees2createwords.substack.com/embed
Goodreads:
https://www.goodreads.com/author/show/6454477.Juanita_Kees
Book Love Book Club:
https://www.facebook.com/groups/607880523038543

Chapter One

Peta Johnson shivered at the feeling of desertion on the street below her hotel room window. The town was neither growing nor dying but ticking over at its own pace. No different from what it had been in the days when she'd lived here.

Where was Bella? Her little girl would be so scared right now. She'd already seen too much. If Paul harmed her … no, she couldn't afford to think he would. If she gave him what he wanted, Bella would be okay. He resented Peta enough to take his revenge, but surely he wasn't evil enough to harm an innocent child.

The hot sun beat down on the small wheat belt town of Williams, Western Australia. Dust devils swirled around tufts of grass struggling to survive in the red sand. Down in a paddock, sheep lazed in the shade. Main Street meandered quietly through town, almost empty except for the line of massive gum trees, the monotony of peeling silver bark occasionally broken by the flash of colour of an Illawarra Flame Tree or the purple and green contrast of a Jacaranda. The only sounds filling the air were the buzzing of the bees, the call of a kookaburra and the occasional blast of a road train horn in the distance.

It all looked so peaceful, so normal, yet somewhere out there her little girl was alone with a dangerous, volatile man who could snap at any moment. Being held ransom for a sum he'd named, a reason she wished she didn't know. Cold fingers of fear dragged on her spine at the thought she might never see her daughter alive again.

Paul had never shown interest in attending school functions, let alone picking Bella up from school. Nothing he'd said or done had ever hinted at him snatching Bella in such a cruel and desperate attempt at blackmail. Not when he'd chosen to merely tolerate her existence.

I'm sorry, Peta. Her father came for her. He said you knew he was picking her up from school today, that it was okay.

It wasn't the grade four teacher's fault. She only had herself to blame. She should have applied sooner for the AVO that would deny Paul access to Bella. And while the process remained tangled up in red tape, he'd taken her.

She hadn't made her divorce from Paul public knowledge. She could imagine the headlines if she did. *Golden Diva splits from Perth's most notorious nightclub owner.* The press would have a field day with the news if they found out, smearing Paul's lies all over the tabloids, dragging her daughter into the damaging spotlight, splashing their personal business all over the news, exposing secrets that were better off staying buried.

If you want to see your daughter alive, bring everything you have to Williams. I mean everything. Don't play games, bitch. You know what I want.

'Bella is safe for now. She's Paul's insurance, he won't hurt her. You have to trust me on that. He has too much at stake.' Her brother's voice interrupted her thoughts.

She rubbed the goosebumps from her skin. 'I wish I could believe that, Mark.' Even with Perth's most awarded detective on Bella's case, she would only believe that once she could hold her daughter again. She turned into his arms and pressed her ear to his chest, listening to the soothing beat of his heart, trying not to count the number of times she'd had to rely on his strength. 'I really want to believe it.'

'I promise I won't let anything happen to Bella. Has anyone ever been hurt on my watch?'

'No. And I hate every moment you put yourself in the firing line to stop it from happening.'

Each day he was out on the street, she dreaded that he too might not come back, and she'd lose everything she had left. Like she'd lost Jaime Caruso when he'd left her to the mercy of a cruel man who'd changed her life for the worst.

But it hurt too much to think about what had happened back then. A lifetime ago. It hurt more to know that, somewhere out there, her daughter was at the mercy of a psychopathic narcissist who needed to be in control more than he needed his next hit.

All her ex-husband had on his mind was to make sure that the security footage of him doing drug deals with outlaw motorcycle gang, Beyond Hell's Reach, and their dirty, scumbag lawyers never surfaced again. Men who used runaway kids as traffickers because it gave them a kick and they wanted to keep on doing it because no one asked questions when the homeless went missing. She shivered.

Mark rubbed warmth into her arms. 'You need to tell Jaime about Bella.'

Peta's heart thudded as she pushed out of his hold. 'No. No way.'

Panic gripped her throat. She was in Caruso territory now. This was Jaime's home town, his turf. Was that why Paul had led her back to Williams? To play a cruel game that would expose the secret she'd fought so hard to keep, force her to confront the past, use her daughter as punishment for always loving Jaime more than him?

And the Carusos had money. Plenty of it. Enough to pay his ransom demands if he asked them for it. Enough to fight her for custody of Bella in court if they knew the truth. Enough to tear her daughter from her arms again either way. She'd fight them every step of the way if they tried. All she wanted was her little girl home and safe.

'He has a right to know.'

'He has no rights.' Frustration and fear-driven anger raged inside her. Every day without finding Bella was a day longer she was at risk. Paul's actions and his commitment to the underworld of crime placed her daughter in a danger so real the consequences didn't bear thinking about. 'Jaime gave up his rights to everything when he left town without even saying goodbye and never bothered to contact me again.' When he'd ignored every attempt of hers to contact him.

'I'm not saying what he did was right, but since then he's spent the last nine years in volatile and remote areas of Afghanistan. Communication with the outside world wasn't high on his list. Survival was. How much longer can you keep it a secret?' Mark checked his watch. 'In about an hour from now you'll be appearing at the shire hall to open the Bushman's Ball. Jaime will be there. Tell him, Peta. Before this blows up in your face. If this deal with Paul goes wrong, everything will be out in the open. Is that the way you want him to find out?'

Her heart raced, blood roared in her ears and

foreboding churned in her stomach. No, she didn't want him to know at all. Nor did she want to appear at the ball, especially now that she knew Jaime would be there. What she wanted was to find her daughter safe, alive and well, then get the hell out of the town that had destroyed her life. To get as far away as possible from Paul Price and the underworld that threatened her and Bella's lives every day and start a new life with a new identity where her child would be safe from Paul Price, his buddies, *and* the Carusos.

And this whole idea of pretending everything was normal, that she was in town as a special guest at the ball, the cover they were using so the press didn't get hold of the real story … what was her brother thinking? How could he even suggest something so ludicrous when her world had been turned on its head? Now, when a most precious part of her life had been stolen.

'I'm not opening the ball. My daughter is missing. This is not the right time for me to be out there pretending everything is normal.'

'You want to break cover? Now? When we're so close to contact with Paul.' Mark shook his head, a furrow forming between his eyebrows. 'It's not going to happen, Peta. We have to go through with this. In fact, this is the perfect time to be out there performing as usual. If you don't see this through, the press will be all over you like blue-arsed flies for failing to appear and your name — The Golden Diva's name — will be mud with the social media trolls for letting this town down. And then the truth about what happened to Bella will have to come out.'

Damn him for being right. That was how Detective Mark Johnson's mind worked. Failure wasn't in his vocabulary. Tenacity his middle name. A skill he'd honed to make him both a formidable enemy and a trustworthy ally. It depended on whose side you were on. She was glad she had him on hers.

Still, she crossed her arms and eyed him defiantly. There had to be another way. Some way where she didn't run the risk of bumping into Jaime Caruso and where the eyes of the whole town wouldn't be on her, waiting to see her reaction having been privy to her emotional breakdown ten years before. The thing with small towns was everyone knew your business. And remembered it.

'This is one time I can't let you back down, Peta.'

He rubbed a hand across his face, the stubble on his chin. The week of strain and lack of sleep had drawn tired lines on his face. She regretted being the reason they were there at all, but at least with Mark in charge of the investigation, there was a glimmer of hope at finding her daughter alive and unharmed. He wouldn't let anyone get away with putting the niece he loved so much in danger, especially not Paul and the people he was involved with.

'All I'm asking is that you keep with the cover

we've arranged and sing at the dance tonight. Let's not waste the resources we've put into this case so far. Sitting holed up in this hotel room won't help us find Bella any quicker. Any changes to the plan can make things go wrong, and then all the hard work we've put in will be undone.'

'I can't, Mark. Not while Paul has my baby. And not when Jaime —' Not when appearing at the ball would bring her face to face with the man she still loved despite what he'd done in the past. Certainly not when she was beside herself with worry for her child, the one it was so important to keep secret from the town's most powerful and influential family. She'd already lost too much.

Peta turned back to the window. Heat shimmered up off the pavement below, warming the glass. She rubbed at her chest to ease away the pain that stabbed at her heart. She'd tried so desperately to bury the memories along with the lies and deceit that lay simmering in the dust, waiting to be stirred up again.

Memories of Jaime and those sultry summer nights. Their wild youth, her naïve belief in happy-ever-afters, and the painful partings when reality beckoned. She didn't want to remember. Nor did she want to have to face the past that had burned a hole in her heart and destroyed her dreams.

'I'm here to find my daughter. Not for business, not for promotion and definitely not for fun. I have to concentrate on finding Bella and getting her home safely. That's all I want from this town. And then I want to leave and never come back here again.'

'Peta …' Mark's comforting hands rested gently on her shoulders as he drew her back into a hug. 'You have to do this. There is no choice. Don't you want this stand-off to be over? Hasn't Paul controlled you for long enough? I want his arse in jail, and this is the best way to make it happen.'

'He told me to stay out of the spotlight. He hates to be disobeyed.' Peta dashed a tear away from her lashes. 'You've seen the terrible things he's capable of. What if he hurts Bella?'

'It's not like you're going on national television or hosting a massive concert. He won't hurt Bella. She's too valuable as a bargaining tool. He wants that evidence a lot more, I promise you that. Stick with the plan. It fits perfectly. All the band is asking for is one gig with the girl from their small town who hit the top of the charts internationally. No one will ever know the real reason you're making this appearance tonight.'

'What if it all goes wrong and they do find out?' Peta lifted her head, a headache starting a slow pound behind her eyes. 'Imagine what the social media trolls would say to that. They'll think it insensitive and shallow of me to perform while my child is missing.'

'We'll do everything we can to keep Bella's disappearance out of the media, you know that. We've had to so we don't compromise the investigation into Paul using the nightclub as a cover for his illegal activities.' Mark raised her chin and looked her squarely in the eye. 'This is a charity event. It's good for the town to have someone as successful as you are opening the Bushman's Ball.'

'Success?' Peta scoffed bitterly. 'Look at the cost of it. My daughter now has a price on her head.' She pushed out of his arms again.

Success should be celebrated. The mantle above her fireplace lined with Grammys and ARIAs paid testament to her achievements. The walls of her city penthouse apartment were decorated with singles that had gone platinum and gold. She'd worked hard for that so-called fame, paid a higher price for it than she'd ever expected to, and carried the weight of it on her shoulders.

She owed the successes *and* the failures to Paul Price; her ex-husband, the man who'd come to her rescue and picked up the pieces after that awful summer. It should have been a dream come true, instead it had stretched into a never-ending nightmare with no way to escape.

Peta shook her head. 'I can't do it. It feels wrong. If something happens to Bella while I'm out there …'

Mark sighed and tugged at her hands until she turned to face him. 'This will mean so much to those people out there who love you. These are the people who helped you achieve your dreams. Just for tonight, help them fulfil their own.'

'I don't know, Mark. What if Paul's out there, watching? If he does something to endanger the lives of the people of this town, I'll never forgive myself.'

'He won't. His fight isn't with them. I wouldn't encourage you to do this if I thought anyone was in danger.'

'I know you're right, but …'

There was a release she found in music despite the pain it brought with it. But with Bella out there at the mercy of a madman, the rules had changed. She was nothing more than a pawn in Paul's game. This wasn't a stage where the show had to go on. This was a reality so cruel it made you wonder at the existence of God.

But she owed it to Mark not to blow their cover. He'd put his own life on hold for her many times. He hadn't bargained on having to protect his sister from a monster driven by jealousy and greed. She owed it to Bella to do everything she could to end this nightmare and get her home safely.

Maybe it was time to face Jaime Caruso too, and the memories she'd locked away in her heart. Jaime whose abandonment had delivered her right into Paul's trap and condemned her to a life in hell. She'd already lost so much. If she lost Bella, she'd have nothing left.

'All right, let's do it.'

'That's the Johnson spirit right there.' Mark hugged

her tightly. 'I've got to go and check in with security and make sure the local cops have been briefed on the real situation. Try to get some rest while I'm away? I know you're not sleeping.'

'How can I? Every time I close my eyes, I see her at Paul's mercy. She must be so scared, Mark.'

'I know,' he said, releasing her. 'I promise you it will all be over soon. I'm doing everything I can to make it happen.' With a reassuring pat on her shoulder, he called out to his partner, Detective Harold Jones, 'I'm leaving, mate. Tag, you're it.' He crossed the room and left, closing the door behind him.

She prayed Mark was right. That this nightmare would end soon. That they could close the door on Paul Price's cell and lock him away forever. She'd unleashed a monster on this tight-knit community, a ticking time bomb with a short fuse and a long memory.

How could the man who had claimed to love her be so cruel? Paul had always known her heart belonged to Jaime and when he couldn't change that, he'd chosen to punish her for it physically, mentally and emotionally. With each blow that fell on her arms, legs or back, he'd remind her why.

Jaime had walked out of her life leaving her alone, lost, pregnant and scared. No call, no messages. Only a silence that screamed with unanswered questions. Now all she had left of his memory was Bella; her life and the thorn in Paul's side.

Everything always came back to Jaime and this town. She'd come full circle. There was a time when life had been free of complications and greed, when love had been passionate and driven. A time when she'd believed in happy endings.

At a bush dance much like the one planned for tonight, she'd been destined to meet two very powerful, yet very different men. One would break her heart, the other would destroy her soul. Both would change her life forever.

Chapter Two

Lieutenant-Colonel Jaime Caruso, formerly of the RAA's 17th Air Land Regiment, stood at the bar looking at the small crowd around him. He'd rather parachute naked into an active war zone. Fitting back into civilian life was proving harder than he'd thought.

Dealing with the open friendliness of small towns differed greatly from the close-knit, high-level security of his desert commando. Learning to communicate at a social level again was challenging. Training himself not to react to sounds like backfiring exhausts, thinking they were gunshots, even harder. Coming back to Williams and trying to fit in again? Mission impossible.

Not that he had a problem with the people. He just hadn't figured on having to come back to this town that raised bittersweet memories of why he'd left it in the first place, and dealing with the question he didn't want to face. *Have you seen Peta yet?*

Not much had changed since he'd been away. The residents had just grown older. Some had left town for bigger and better things, others had stayed to raise their own children in the same small town family environment they'd grown up in.

Not exactly the lifestyle he'd had on his agenda. Plans changed, like now. He'd chosen to give up his military career to help his father. Go with the plan to move the mining operations office from Williams to Perth, where Dad could continue to receive the best medical care possible for his cancer. For Jaime to take over the reins of a company he'd never wanted to run but would because his father's life depended on it now.

Jaime thought he'd shaken the dust of this town from his shoes a lifetime ago. Coming back opened doors he'd rather keep shut.

Peta Johnson is not the girl for you. Maria will be waiting when you're ready. She's practically family already. A much better choice of wife. She will stand by you because she knows the ropes. You need to concentrate on running the family business.

He grimaced at the memory of his father's words. Running was what he did best. He'd run hard and fast from the prospect of marriage to someone he didn't love, managing a business he didn't want, and joined the military instead. The only way he could stop himself from ruining a young girl's dreams.

Jaime cracked open the beer he didn't really want but needed to keep his hands busy, and sipped the cold, yeasty brew. He hadn't attended the annual Bushman's Ball for a long time, but when Mark had told him Peta would be opening the show tonight, he hadn't been able to resist coming to see the girl he'd had to leave behind.

Anger, regret, too many emotions he'd buried for so long pushed to the surface as he returned waved greetings, shook hands and made small talk with the people of the town he'd grown up in. Jaime sighed as a jolt to his elbow sent his beer spilling onto his shoes. It was just too crowded, damn it, and he felt like an alien in his own home town.

He allowed himself an amused grin as he surveyed the shire hall. The community had pulled out all the stops as usual. Bluey Mack and Bill Gorey stood on guard at the door on alert for any nasty surprises like gate crashers, just as they had at the annual dances for as long as he could remember. Their sleepy town would be in no danger tonight. As long as the two old blokes stayed away from the pokies in the pub next door.

Movement near the entrance caught his eye and an excited murmur rippled through the crowd. Jaime's grip tightened around the beer bottle as he caught sight of

Peta's auburn head close to Mark's shoulder. The crowd closed in around them. He ignored the misstep of his heartbeat as a smile lit her face, her features becoming animated in conversation.

Oh God, he remembered that smile well. And the life it brought to her eyes. It was that smile that had won his heart back then, the one that still haunted his thoughts today. The one he'd missed so terribly since he'd closed the door on her one last time.

They moved across the hall. People milled about her, dealing out hugs and welcome homes, holding out autograph books, posters and T-shirts for signing. He smiled. She deserved the success. She'd earned the happiness he'd never been able to give her. But, Jesus, it hurt to know that she'd found that happiness with someone else.

No point living in the past. He tore his gaze from her and looked around. The ladies of the Country Women's Association manned their refreshment stalls and finished off last minute decorations. A group of farmers gathered in a corner near the door, discussing crops, rain and the increasing impact of the growth of the mine on farming.

Pastor McLean's wife stepped forward and blocked Peta's progress in his direction. Within earshot. Only a few steps away. Irritation trickled up Jaime's spine to mingle with relief. He'd thought he was ready to face her. Perhaps not.

'Hello, Peta. It's been years since we saw you last. This is such a lovely surprise. Thank you so much for agreeing to sing for us tonight.' Mrs McLean pulled her into a hug. 'We're all so excited to have you home. Come along, dear. We'll get you something to drink.'

Releasing his hold on her, Mark let Mrs McLean lead Peta away to the refreshments table where she was surrounded by CWA ladies, then stepped forward to stand next to Jaime and scan the crowd.

Jaime frowned. He understood his long-time friend's protectiveness of his famous sister, but there was a tension to his shoulders and a watchfulness in his eyes that said DSS Mark Johnson was on duty.

'Expecting trouble?' Jaime shook his friend's outstretched hand firmly.

'What makes you think that?' Mark stood next to him and cast a slow, deceptively idle look around the room.

'You're assessing. You've homed in on a few unfamiliar faces then dismissed them. And it's not every day one of Perth's finest plays bodyguard to a nightclub diva whether she's family or not.'

'Retired nightclub diva.' Mark's smile was more of a grimace. 'As observant as always, I see.'

'Call it a trained eye. Your edge gets edgier every time I see you. Is there something I need to know about tonight?'

Mark shrugged, another deceptively easy move and

a dead giveaway that something had him on high alert because his poker face was firmly in place. 'Nope.'

'Right.' Jaime drawled the word as he picked at the label on his beer bottle. 'If you say so. How's she doing?'

'Not so good.'

Jaime shook his head. He'd wanted her to be happy even though the thought made him miserable. But he'd done what he'd had to do. 'Anything I need to know about?'

'Not right now.'

He pushed back the disappointment that crept into his soul. Of course she wouldn't need him anymore. She'd got on with her life, made it a success, perhaps even forgotten about what they'd once shared. And he only had himself to blame for that. He'd been the one to walk away. 'Okay, I get the picture.'

Mark sighed. 'I'm afraid you don't. There are things I can't explain right now. Things happening that I wish weren't.' He waved at Peta as town mayor, Allan Brookefield, escorted her on stage.

She waved back and for a split-second Jaime saw her gaze rest on him before she turned away. Disappointment churned in his gut. He deserved to be ignored. He deserved every bit of rejection she threw his way.

'Fair enough.'

He didn't want to be here, however much he'd

enjoyed the catch up with the townsfolk. It had been a long time since he'd ventured back to Williams and even longer before he would again. Perth would be his home now. At least there nothing reminded him of Peta. Here every street corner, the shade of the trees down by the river, the coffee shop on Main Street — all of it brought back memories of the girl he'd let go while he still loved her.

Allan Brookefield stepped up to the mike to deliver his welcome speech. 'And we're very honoured to have a special guest with us tonight. Ladies and gentlemen, please welcome back to Williams, the lovely Peta Johnson!'

The lights dimmed and the spotlight centred on Peta as she launched into an energetic performance of popular country songs before slowing the pace. He heard the tension in her voice, saw the sadness that filled her eyes and noted the way her shoulders rounded under the weight of her emotions. And damned if he didn't feel every ounce of her pain echoing through him.

'Here's one I wrote myself. You might recognise it,' she said.

Her voice floated over Jaime as she sang. Drawing him in, entangling him in the same passion that had the audience riveted to their seats. The dancers on the floor stood still. The magic of her voice flowed through the hall, engulfing it in the emotions she created as she sang the song that had rocketed her to fame.

As the song drew to an end, Mark stood quietly at Jaime's elbow. 'She needs you, Jaime. Now more than ever.'

He looked at Mark. 'I don't need to know why. It won't make any difference. It's too late. We had no chance then and even less of a chance now. I have nothing she wants.' It hurt to say the words aloud, ripped through his gut like a fishing knife, but it was no less than the truth.

Mark leaned closer. 'I can't tell you everything, but she's been through a rough time before and after the divorce from Paul. She could use a friend.'

'That's the one thing we can never be again, even if she wanted it.' Jaime closed his eyes and sighed. 'It really doesn't matter anymore, Mark. Her divorce doesn't make a difference to what could have been.' Even if the knowledge made his heart beat a little faster. 'I can't change the past.'

Mark shook his head. 'That's where you're wrong. It's only dead and buried in your books. But that's for you to decide. She's staying at the Williams Hotel, Suite 201,' he said, turning to walk away. 'And I'm only letting you have that information because I trust you not to share it.'

Taking a deep, steadying breath, Jaime turned back towards the girl on the stage. She wore the same little black dress she'd worn when he'd met her years before. It fit a little more snugly now that her slender curves had matured. Her chestnut hair shone under the lights as she slowed the pace again. He remembered the glittering green eyes which had once seared his soul, the dusting of freckles on the pert nose he used to kiss, and the smooth, almost translucent skin on the cheeks he used to touch.

Slowly he moved forward to get a closer look at the woman who had filled his dreams and thoughts constantly for as long as he could remember. He'd put it down to guilty conscience that she'd haunted him for so long because he didn't dare consider the other option.

She sang with her soul. The song was meant for someone special. Her ex-husband perhaps, he thought with all too familiar feelings of jealousy. From this close he could see the dampness at the corners of her beautiful green eyes as she sang, pouring her heart into the performance. It was this ability to engage emotion that had kept her steady in the Top Ten on the music charts. He could understand why recording studios worldwide had fallen over themselves to sign her up, why they were devastated when she'd announced she was retiring from the music scene.

Dear God, he'd never thought it possible she could be more beautiful than he remembered, but she was. Tightness gripped his heart, squeezing painfully. He swallowed around the lump in his throat.

As he stood at the base of the stage staring up at her, she looked down. Their eyes met and held. He heard her voice falter before she tore her eyes from his and moved away across the stage. Jaime felt his heart plummet from his chest down into his stomach. He didn't want to feel this way. He shouldn't love her after all this time. His lips tightened as he took one last look at her and strode from the hall.

Peta stared down at Jaime's departing back, her heart pounding. Even though Mark had warned her he'd be there, it hadn't softened the blow. And it made singing the song she'd written for him so much more personal with him standing there, still as darkly gorgeous as ever.

Pain, deep and sharp, seized her heart and her voice faltered, the words of the song blurring in her mind. Desperately she tried to regain her concentration and banish him from her thoughts. She couldn't let herself be caught up in the magic he weaved again, no way she could think about second chances. No room for love when his daughter was in danger.

Mark was right. Jaime deserved to know about Bella. But what if knowing led to her daughter being taken from her again? It was her fault for staying with an abusive Paul for as long as she had, for letting him take Bella so easily. With her past and the reputation Paul had brought to The Golden Diva nightclub, it wouldn't be hard for the Carusos to prove her an unfit mother.

Waves of dizziness threatened her concentration, played havoc with her pitch. It was a mistake to come back to this town. She'd avoided the place for so long, dreading this moment, anticipating this reaction. She hated Paul for forcing her to come back here, for dragging her daughter into the middle of his messed-up life. More than all that, she hated herself for letting it happen.

As Jaime slammed through the rear door of the hall, she felt her heart shatter again, the same way it had all those years ago. Part of her wanted to run after him, but she knew she wouldn't. She didn't deserve answers.

As quickly as she could, she finished her rendition and thanked the audience, leaving them shouting for more. Her mind reeled as she left the stage and felt Mark's hand at her elbow, saw the grim set of his mouth.

'I'll take you back to your room.'

'Bugger off. You've done enough.' The words hitched in her throat, anger vying for attention with gut-wrenching pain.

'I'm not letting you walk back to the hotel alone, so don't even think of doing a runner on me.'

Peta pulled out of his hold. 'I'm angry, not stupid.'

Her voice rose an octave, drawing the attention of onlookers. There'd be whispers, well-meaning ones, of the moment Peta Johnson had come face-to-face with her past before he'd walked out the door on her again. She reigned in her temper and turned to walk as quickly as she could through the crowd without ignoring the friendly outstretched hands and pats on the shoulder.

Behind her, Mark kept silent but close. She allowed him to follow only because beyond the doors of the hall, danger might lurk only steps away.

Chapter Three

Jaime sat on the riverbank, his back to the tree and his legs stretched out in front of him, tossing pebbles into the water. The place that had once brought him peace had him on edge tonight.

This spot he and Peta had once shared now only held memories that filled him with regret. The water flowing over the river stones no longer soothed his irritability as it had in the past. At least not tonight.

Damn Mark for his meddling. Peta was back and the mere sight of her had his head spinning. He'd thought he'd managed to securely package her away in that place in his heart he never wanted to explore again, because it made him realise how much he'd lost. What he'd thrown away.

He rubbed a hand across his chin, feeling the

roughness of a day's growth. She'd been so young then, and innocent. Too innocent not to be burned by the fire that had raged so strongly between them. Too young to be so consumed by passion. Heat that even years after he'd been with her, still made him want to take her in his arms and kiss away the wrongs, the doubts, the fears.

Her adult life had only just begun the night they'd first made love out on a blanket under this tree with the stars bright above them. She hadn't known anyone but him, hadn't explored her choices beyond the boundaries of the town she'd grown up in. Peta was made for babies, white picket fences and promises of happy-ever-afters. Just not with him. He hadn't been anywhere near ready for long term commitment. Here he was, still trying to outrun it.

Tossing the last pebble, Jaime stood, dusted off his pants, and walked back to his car. He had to see her. Just once more. Talk to her to explain why he'd done what he did. Maybe then there'd be closure.

Closure? Who was he kidding? Standing there looking up at her on stage tonight; the attraction, the spark between them was still there. No way he'd mistaken it.

Jaime pressed the button on his key remote and listened to the whirr of the mechanism unlocking the doors, loud in the silence. He raised his head slowly. Too quiet. Unnaturally so. Not even the usual singing of the frogs in the air. Unease trickled down his spine, the sense of being watched raising the hairs on his neck. He knew that feeling too well. It stank of ambush. He turned, peered into the shadows along the riverbank. Nothing.

This was Williams for God's sake. What had he expected? The most dangerous thing in town was Bill Gorey's toothless old dog who had arthritis and seldom moved from his sunny spot on the veranda. Still the uncomfortable itch between his shoulder blades grew. Perhaps it was Mark's edginess rubbing off on him.

He pulled open the driver's door, leaned on it to scan the bushland that hugged the riverbank and the gumtrees beyond it. Empty. Disquiet curled in his stomach. Something was definitely off. An eerie silence lurked across the water, the trees whisper-quiet in the still of the night. And then he heard the thud of shoes softened by the grass, felt the presence, but had no time to turn around and face it before a sharp searing pain bit into his skull, hard enough to blur his vision. Something blunt. The butt of a gun?

Pulled back by his neck, his attacker threw him to the ground, jarring bones and bruising muscles. A hefty weight latched onto his back as he sprawled face-first on the sandy ground with his hands trapped at his sides, and a meaty hand clamped tightly over his mouth. Cruel fingers dragged his head back, wrenching the muscles in his neck. Cold, hard steel glinted in the dim light of the moon.

'You bastard. Stay away from my wife.'

Jesus Christ. Pain needled his scalp as his attacker tightened his grip.

'I've lived with your ghost for ten long fucking years.'

Paul Price. It had to be. He hadn't messed with anyone else's wife. The knife point pricked at his neck. Jaime tried to free his hands, but Paul's weight held him down. He had to get away. The press of the blade sharpened, burning at his throat. Peta's ex meant business. When had the man turned feral?

'I should just kill you now.' Paul's breath was hot and ugly in his ear, the weight easing a little as he leaned over. 'How would the princess feel about that, do you think? Or maybe I should just kill you both and finish this for good.'

No chance. Jaime heaved his body upwards, catching Paul by surprise and dislodging him. The knife cut into Jaime's jaw and Paul's fist connected with his ear, sending pain roaring through his skull. A trickle of blood ran down the skin of his throat. Anger flooded through him. Leaping to his feet, he turned to face his attacker, but the man was on the run and the dizziness in his head and ringing in his ears stopped him from giving chase.

God damn it. Jaime's head pounded as he wiped away the blood on his jaw with his hand. What the hell was going on? If Peta's ex was out of control that would explain Mark's vigilance tonight. Bloody hell, he had no choice but to go and see her now. If nothing else, she owed him an explanation for why her ex-husband wanted to slit his throat.

With a groan, he slid into the driver's seat. His ribs ached and he'd have a few bruises in the morning. Nothing he wasn't used to. Slamming the door closed, he gunned the engine, engaged gears and turned out onto the road to negotiate the winding bends back into town, questions churning in his mind, urgency clawing at his gut. What if Paul turned on Peta with that knife?

Parking the car outside the hotel, he got out and headed through the old jarrah doors. He took the staircase to the hotel rooms quickly, adrenaline running high, his mind sorting through what had happened at the river. Mark would need to know, but first he had to make sure Peta was safe. That Paul hadn't got here before him.

Outside Suite 201, he took a deep breath before knocking. A mountain of a man opened the door, wearing a police jacket and a scowl on his face that would send any sane man running. Jaime had lost his sanity somewhere between the shire hall and the flight of stairs up to Peta's suite, but he knew Harold Jones well enough to know he was in deep shit. Deeper than he already was.

'Hey, Harold.'

'What do you want?' Harold peered at his jaw. 'And what the hell happened to your face?'

It took a lot to intimidate a Caruso, but Mark's detective mate looked angry enough to use the gun in his side holster and Jaime wasn't in the mood to die. Harold's face was all harsh contours and, judging by the angle, his nose had been broken a few times since Jaime had seen him last. The combination made him look like a hawk, ready to rip its prey to shreds.

'Explanations can wait. I need to see Peta first.'

'She doesn't want to see you.'

'Please. I need to see she's okay,' he tried again, taking a step forward and pulling himself up to his full height. He hadn't survived gruelling manoeuvres and years of facing down the enemy not to take advantage of his size.

Harold looked as if he'd like to hurl him down the stairs he'd just climbed. 'I'm here. She's okay. We don't need you.'

As the door began to close on him, Jaime put his hand out to stop it. 'Mark thinks she does. He told me to come.' He froze as Peta appeared at the detective's side.

'It's all right, Harold,' she said quietly. 'Let him in, I'll talk to him.'

Harold hesitated a little longer. 'Are you sure, Peta? I wouldn't mind throwing him out on his arse.'

He flexed muscles Jaime had no doubt could easily carry out the threat and have his arse hurting for months.

'I'm sure. Give us a couple of minutes, okay? If he puts one foot wrong, I'll let you toss him out.'

Harold narrowed his eyes but stepped aside to clear the doorway. 'You have five minutes, Caruso. Use them well. They might be your last.'

'Thanks.' His dry tone earned him another scowl.

Peta turned to walk back into the room. 'Come inside, Jaime. You look as if you need a drink,' she said. 'And that cut needs seeing to. What did you do?'

Adrenaline gave way to anger. 'I had a little run in with your ex-husband and a knife.' Jaime followed her inside.

Harold paused in his scan of the corridor. 'Say what?'

Peta stopped and turned around. Her gaze shot to Harold's, the sharp intake of her breath and the little shiver she gave a dead giveaway that she knew exactly who he'd run into.

'Where?' Harold's voice thundered through the room.

'Down by the river.'

'The bastard. This is a game changer. I'll call Mark.'

'Great. You do that. And then I'd like to know why someone I've never met wants to kill me.'

With a dark look at Jaime, Harold stepped outside and closed the door behind him, leaving them alone in the room. Jaime watched Peta pour him a whisky at the bar, her hand not quite steady. Anger dissolved into concern. He breathed in her perfume, the scent bringing back sweet memories of her in his arms, of the promises he'd whispered and failed to keep. If things had worked out differently, would she still be in danger now? And he had no doubt that she was in danger.

Peta held out the glass to him. He took it from her, their fingers touching. For a brief moment he held her gaze until she moved away before he could read her thoughts, but he'd seen enough to recognise the fear in her eyes. He'd seen it over and over in the eyes of the men, women and children fleeing the terror that haunted their world every day.

The sensations that ran up his arm from her fleeting touch came as no surprise. Time had definitely not lessened his reaction to her. Taking a deep breath, he let it out on a whoosh. They had reality to deal with first.

'I guess there's no need for me to ask why there is a police detective answering your door. What happened to turn a good man bad, Peta?' He tried to remember what he knew about Paul. Not much except that he'd been the powerhouse driving Peta's success in the music industry, fulfilling the dreams he never could. Paul Price had come to town after he'd left.

'That's where he had everyone fooled. Paul was never a good man, just very good at playing the role.' Peta lifted a finger to touch a spot next to the congealed blood on his chin. 'We need to clean that cut. What did he do?'

'He ambushed me down by the river. The bastard took me by surprise. Got the knife in, tried to blow out my eardrums and then disappeared.' Jaime grimaced. No point sugar-coating it for her. She'd know what she was up against. A man that aggressive wouldn't be picky about who he took his fists to. That he might have used those hands to hurt Peta, made Jaime see red. 'He was gone by the time I got to my feet.'

'Oh God, Jaime, I'm so sorry. Paul could have killed you.'

Her hand came up to cover her mouth and he read the raw fear in her eyes. He'd never been a betting man, but right now he'd bet there was more to this than a pissed-off husband stalking his ex-wife.

'I don't think it was his intention to kill, only to scare me off.' Any sane man would be scared off, but he'd seen far more frightening things during his years of service in the military. 'If he really wanted to slit my throat, he wouldn't have wasted time talking and he wouldn't have run away when I shook him off. He would have stayed to fight.'

Peta shivered. 'Yes, he's never been good at dealing with people who fight back. I'm so sorry you had to get involved, Jaime. Look at you. He could have done so much damage.'

'Well, luckily he didn't.' Jaime winced as she touched the base of the cut on his jawline.

'Looks deep enough to leave a scar.' Quickly she

drew her hand away. 'Come into the bathroom. I'll clean it up for you,' she said.

He followed her across the suite into the bathroom and sat down on the edge of the bath. Peta ran water into the basin, reached up into the cupboard and pulled out a first aid kit. He watched her methodical movements as she arranged the contents of the kit on the vanity and tried to put together the pieces of what had happened down at the river. He needed answers.

'What's going on, Peta?'

Dipping a cotton pad in the lukewarm water in the basin, she swabbed at his jaw to clean away the blood. 'Not now.' Tossing the pad into the trash, she picked up the disinfectant.

Jaime watched as she dripped some of the contents of the bottle into a plastic kidney dish. Her hands still shook a little. No doubt in his mind that she was scared shitless, and so she should be. 'What's wrong with now?'

'I need to process.' She dabbed a cotton bud into the mixture and then onto the cut.

'Ouch.' Jaime jerked back at the sting of the liquid meeting raw flesh.

'Don't be a baby.'

Stepping into the V of his legs, she placed a gentle hand on the back of his head to ease him forward again, her fingers sinking into his hair. An unexpected fizz of pleasure rippled through him. The feel of her hands against his scalp, the way her fingers weaved through his hair reminded him of another time, a happier time when actions like this had led to more. Jaime covered her free hand with his, removing the cotton bud and placing it in the basin.

'I'm afraid for you.' He folded her fingers into her palm, rubbing his thumb across her knuckles.

Peta drew in a sharp breath. She tried to wriggle away, but he couldn't overlook the shiver that had run through her at his touch or the flash of heat in her eyes. No, she wasn't immune to him at all. That shouldn't make him happy. Not when there was a threat to her life and now his too. He cupped her hand lightly in his, giving her the option to go or to stay. She stayed.

'You don't have to be. I have Mark and Harold. Go, Jaime. This isn't any of your business.'

'Your husband made it my business today.'

Her shoulders stiffened. 'My *ex*-husband. There are things you don't know.'

He hooked his arm around her waist and eased her down to sit on his thigh. 'Then tell me.' If he held onto her he could keep her safe, protect her from whatever it was she faced, like he should have before instead of running away. She leaned against him for a moment. Her forehead pressed into his neck, so he folded her into his arms and hugged her closer.

'I can't. Not yet.' She pushed away and when he

opened his mouth to protest, she pressed a finger to his lips. 'Not yet.'

He wanted to kiss the sadness from her eyes, the pinch from her lips and ease away the pain of everything he'd allowed to happen to her. 'But soon?'

She nodded. 'After you've spoken to Mark.'

Standing, she began packing the unused items back into the first aid kit, leaving Jaime wondering how it was his arms felt empty without her. They always had. No one had ever been able to fill that space the same way Peta had. A few had tried, and when the adrenaline had been running high and he didn't know if the next day would be his last, he'd let them. But it was Peta's face he saw when he closed his eyes.

'We have a lot to talk about. I owe you an explanation.' He tried to sound casual as his heart thundered in his chest.

Peta seemed totally unmoved by his words. Cool, calm and collected now, unlike the pain and panic he'd seen in her eyes earlier. 'You don't owe me anything. You came, you left, we grew up.'

Clearly she hadn't forgotten what had happened between them, nor had she forgiven him. He watched the shutters come down and the walls go up as she closed him out. The gentle hands that had tended his cut now moved quickly to clean up. Tension straightened the spine that had softened in his arms only moments ago.

He stood, the small bathroom making keeping his distance challenging. This close, he could see the tired lines around her eyes, the bruised look above her cheekbones from lack of sleep. Whatever was going on, it was keeping her awake at night.

She turned and left the bathroom. He followed her into the small sitting area in silence. Peta sat on the sofa and patted the seat next to her.

'Sit down, Jaime. I'm sure Mark will be here soon to take your statement about what happened at the river.'

Jaime cast a glance at Harold who was reading the paper and pretending he wasn't keeping a close eye on him. 'You have two high-ranking detectives playing bodyguard and an ex-husband on the loose brandishing a knife. How is it you're taking this so calmly?'

'They're on a case.' Peta sighed, despair reflected in her eyes. 'And I'm not calm about this at all.'

'A case. Yet clearly they're protecting you. When Paul Price baled me up tonight, he threatened to kill us both. I take that very seriously.'

Peta grimaced. 'I can't give you details, Jaime. I have my reasons.'

'Which are?'

'None of your business.'

She was right. She wasn't his business anymore. But being here with her tonight, being threatened by her ex — it made him realise that the door on their past wasn't closed as tightly as he'd thought.

Chapter Four

Peta waited as Jaime sat down next to her, looking increasingly annoyed. He hadn't changed much except for the touches of premature grey peppering his dark hair, the short military-style cut making him sexier than ever. Lines fanned out from the corners of his eyes and his mouth had tightened to a grim line. Good. Better he stayed angry with her. That way he wouldn't be tempted to hang around and couldn't get dragged into this any further. He could leave as soon as he'd reported Paul's attack on him. Get out of town.

Paul's attack. That thought shot a red-hot arrow through her heart. If his behaviour had escalated, Bella could be in very real danger and all Mark's reassurances about her being safe could be dead wrong. Panic rose in her throat. Every motherly instinct she'd honed over the years screamed for her to react. Only the fact that she had the best people taking care of the investigation stopped her. Hard as it was, she had to trust her brother's instincts too.

A frown formed on Jaime's brow. Her hands itched to smooth it from his handsome face. The contoured jaw, the grooved line that appeared when he smiled, the full, deliciously curved lips that had once held hers … every nerve-end remembered how his skin had felt against hers.

Need, desire, anger and rejection warred for attention inside her. So long ago, yet still she loved him. People changed. Did he deserve to know the truth? She wasn't sure he did. And if he did find out the truth, she stood to lose her most precious gift all over again.

Jaime shifted on the seat next to her and the material of his trousers tightened across his thighs. Peta looked away, not wanting to feel the warmth of attraction that should be long dead, blossom through her. She remembered those strong thighs well; the flex of the muscles under her hands, the way they'd clenched around hers. But that was in the past and the future wasn't hers to contemplate. Her daughter was, and always would be, her first priority.

'So, how have you been, Jaime?' Better to bring things back to a friendly level, even though they'd never be friends again. Anything to stop him asking questions she hadn't yet worked up the courage to answer. Not when she wasn't prepared for it. And talk took the edge off. 'Mark told me you were in Afghanistan. Are you home on leave?'

Jaime's lips tightened more for a moment, his voice taking on an impatient edge when he finally answered. 'You really want to talk about me? Now?'

'Humour me.' With every moment he sat next to her, her resolve to keep her daughter's parentage a secret weakened. This nightmare had to end somewhere. The reasons Paul had taken Bella in the first place needed to be revealed. Mark was right. Jamie deserved to know about his daughter, but she had to be prepared for the consequences. And right now, she wasn't prepared for anything except to fight for Bella's life with everything she had.

'Fine, we'll do it your way. I've taken an honourable discharge from the military. Dad's cancer meant I had to come back to take over the reins at the mine and move the office to the city, closer to the oncology unit. I've been back a little over three months, mostly looking for premises to set up office in. We've found one in the Mutual Investments building in West Perth.'

'I'm sorry to hear about your dad's illness.' A little shiver crept up her spine. So close. She knew the office complex he meant, could see the high rise that would house Caruso Coal Mining's head office from the terrace of her penthouse apartment, never thought he might have an office there. Why would he need one when he was off risking his life in a war he'd chosen freely to go fight?

She'd walked past the building with Bella a few times. At any time in the future, they could run into each other, and he would know without a doubt whose daughter Bella was. If Paul's violence escalated, Jaime may never have the opportunity to know her at all. She swallowed against the pain that thought brought with it.

Jaime looked at her. 'I can almost hear those thoughts churning, Peta. I don't know what it is you're not telling me, but I hope you'll trust me enough when you decide to. I thought you'd left Williams behind, traded the red dust for the bright lights of the city.'

Peta stiffened. Hadn't that been her biggest mistake to date? The bright lights were the reason she was back, sitting here now with the man she'd resigned herself to love but never see again, the root cause of her daughter being in the hands of a dangerous madman on the verge of destroying everything she lived for.

'Not everything works out the way we want it to.' She looked away so he wouldn't see the pain in her eyes. 'This situation with Paul ...'

Peta broke off as her mobile phone rang, vibrating on the coffee table. She flew up off the sofa, her arms hugging her waist, her heart pounding, too scared to move closer to check the caller ID and unable to keep the panic from her voice. If this was Paul, Jaime would know the truth because she'd have to put it on speaker. 'Harold—'

Harold dropped the newspaper and checked the number on the screen. 'It's your mother. Want me to get it?'

'No. No, it's okay. I'll take it.' Peta swallowed the mixture of fear and disappointment, picked up the phone and, pressing her fingertips to her closed lids to stem the sting of tears, answered. 'Hello, Mum.'

'Have you heard anything yet?'

There was no concern in her voice, only harsh, unspoken accusation. Peta wondered at how cold her mother had become. The years had not been kind to any of them.

'Not yet. We're still waiting for a phone call,' Peta responded. 'As soon as we have more news, I'll let you know.'

'All this nonsense is your fault, Peta. You had no reason to leave Paul in the first place. None of this would have happened if you hadn't still been hankering after Jaime Caruso.'

Peta's shoulders stiffened. Her mother didn't know the half of it. She and Mark had kept the truth from her as much as they could. Margaret Johnson had always been blinded by Paul's charm. He'd never been capable of any wrong in her eyes.

'I can't really talk about it right now. Can I ring you back a little later, Mum? I have a visitor.'

Mrs Johnson muttered, 'Typical. Flitting about while your marriage is in tatters. Have you no concern for your husband and child? Stop this nonsense, Peta. Paul's only doing this because he wants you back, and it's where you belong. You owe it to him after all he's done for you and … the child.'

Her mother hardly ever referred to Bella by name. How could a grandmother not love and accept her for the beautiful child she was? How could she not want to hug and treasure the little girl who brought light to Peta's otherwise dark world?

'We've been through this. I've got to go now.'

'Who's there with you? Who is it?'

Peta closed her eyes and sighed. She anticipated her mother's reaction and pressed a hand to her churning stomach. 'It's Jaime, Mum.'

'Jaime Caruso!' Her mother's disgust rang in her ears. 'What does he want? I thought you were well rid of him after what he did to you. You tell him to leave right this minute. He has no business back in your life. You don't need him around right now. And don't tell him about the child.'

Peta wanted to smash the device against the wall, make the call end, make the anger and lies go away. But they couldn't. Not now, not ever. And her mother would never forgive her for coming home pregnant with Jaime Caruso's baby.

'This is not the right time. I need to keep the line

open. We'll talk later. Goodbye,' she answered, cutting her mother short on any further comment.

Frustrated, she pressed the red button to end the call, tossed the phone onto the table and walked over to the window to look out across the lights of the small town. Peta wished that just once her mother could show some warmth, be kind and supportive. God knew, she could use it. For the first time since Bella's disappearance, she let down her guard. She was tired of being strong, tired of the secrets and lies. Tears welled in her eyes. Unable to control them, they spilled softly down her cheeks, dropping onto her hands on the window ledge. She dashed them away.

Jaime moved in beside her, placing a comforting arm around her shoulders. She looked up at him, tears glistening. A strangled sob escaped her lips and Jaime pulled her closer, tucking her head tightly under his chin and resting his cheek against her hair. His arms felt so good … so right.

When her sobs lessened, he wiped the tears away gently and stroked her hair. 'What's going on, Peta?' he asked quietly. 'Why are you here?'

Peta let a sigh shudder through her and gently pushed him away. She couldn't think with him so close, but God help her, she wanted to bury herself in his warmth and strength. Her mind screamed for him to leave while her heart cried out for him to stay and hold her until this mess was over.

Why did he have to show up again? At a time when she didn't have the strength to deal with him. So much for time healing wounds. They'd just been ripped open again. She pulled her shoulders back and straightened. She was a stronger person now. Her mother was right. She only had herself to blame for the mess her life was in.

'I can't involve you, Jaime. You should go now. Mark will come to wherever you're staying to take your statement.'

Telling him about Bella now would only raise more questions. Ones she wasn't ready to answer. She had to close the door on him, shut him out like the stranger he'd become. Because that's exactly what he was … just another stranger in her life. She didn't want him involved in the situation with Paul and Bella. He'd come too close to the truth already. If she didn't let him go, everything she held dear would be in jeopardy. When this nightmare was over and Bella was safe, she'd tell him the truth.

'Harold will show you out.' Peta tried to pull herself together. It would be too easy to confide in Jaime, to rely on his strength, but soon he would be on the move again and she would be back to the struggle for survival, alone except for Mark and Harold.

Jaime had a world of responsibility on the table in Perth and she had Bella to worry about. He would be just another passing memory, for the second time in her life. She picked up his jacket, savouring its warmth, inhaling the smell of his expensive aftershave as she ran her hand across the buttery soft leather before handing it to him. He looked down at her, but she refused to meet his eyes.

'Let me know if there's anything I can do to help you, Peta. Mark knows where to find me. We do need to talk about what happened back then.'

Peta shook her head. 'There's nothing to talk about. You can never bring back the past, Jaime. Let it go.'

Heaviness weighed on her heart. This had to be the goodbye again. It hurt even more because of the circumstances and the time and distance between them.

Jaime sighed and pressed a kiss to her forehead. 'I'll see you around.'

She hugged her arms to her chest to still the ache under her breastbone. 'Jaime …' What point was there in saying sorry? It wouldn't fix a thing. She shook her head. 'Never mind, it doesn't matter.' She turned away. She couldn't possibly watch him walk through the door again.

As she reached the window and the view of the lights on Main Street, the tinted glass erupted in a shattered web. She saw a flash as something whizzed past her head, heard the thump of it hitting a wall, then Harold leaped across the room and dragged her to the ground, yelling at Jaime to get down.

'Stay down until I tell you to get up.' After a few

more moments making sure the danger had passed and no more shots were fired, Harold stood and helped Peta up.

'Are you all right?' he asked, checking her over quickly.

Peta nodded. 'Jaime?' she asked, looking over to where Jaime stood at the door, staring in disbelief at the bullet lodged in the wall next to where he'd stood only moments before.

'Twice in one night. *Jesus*. Could someone please tell me what the hell is going on?' Anger flared in his eyes as they pinned hers.

Harold's grip tightened gently on Peta's arm. 'I promise you'll get your answers, Caruso, but you'll have to wait a little longer. I'll call Mark again. He'll need to bring help,' he said.

Chapter Five

Peta walked over to the liquor cabinet for the second time that night and poured them each a stiff shot of whisky as Harold reached for his phone.

'Drink up,' she said, offering Jaime a glass.

Her hand shook and the whisky sloshed around in the crystal cut glass. He took it from her, his own hands not exactly steady. Gunfire still had the power to set adrenaline on fire in his blood, the danger it brought with it setting his senses on high alert. He tossed back the drink and waited as the warmth eased the chill from his spine. With a hand at Peta's back, he guided her back to sit on the sofa.

What the fuck just happened? Jaime swallowed the fear that rose in his throat. Good God, they could have both been killed. If the assailant had taken the shot when they'd both stood at the window, they'd be dead.

His heart pounded at the wall of his chest. Either the culprit was a poor shot, or he'd aimed to scare not kill. And Jaime didn't need to be Sherlock Holmes to work out who it was after what had happened down by the river. The bastard had followed him back to the hotel for a second go.

Still shaking, Peta swallowed her whisky. Jaime covered her cold hands with his, removing the glass from her fingers. She looked up at him, lips quivering, and he knew he wouldn't be going anywhere. Not with her in this state.

Jaime took her trembling hands in his. 'Don't send me away, Peta. I want to help you. I'll be here for you for as long as you need me. I owe you that much.'

'What can you do that my brother can't?' Peta looked at him. 'When this is over, you'll be off, and I'll have to pick up the pieces alone again. Thanks for the thought, but I'll be fine. Get on with your life, Jaime. Forget I ever existed in it. It's the safest thing to do.'

Jaime thrust a hand through his hair. 'Safe? Your ex-husband is shooting at you, for God's sake. This is a lot worse than running out on you like I did back then.'

'Then why did you?'

Her voice was quiet, but she might as well have shouted at him because it hurt to hear the question from her lips when he'd asked himself the same question time and again.

'I thought I was doing the right thing by leaving you behind. You were so young. You had dreams I didn't want to tread on.' The words rushed out before he could stop them. 'Without me holding you back, you made those dreams come true.'

Peta stared at their hands, still linked. Shaking, she pried her fingers loose and clasped her hands in her lap. 'I was old enough to know what I wanted. Don't be guided by your conscience, Jaime. You don't owe me anything, not even an explanation. Let's just accept that it didn't work out. It wasn't meant to be. You need to go. Now. Please.'

Oh, she was good at making it look like she was pushing him away, but he understood the fear and urgency in her voice. His presence was making Paul's anger worse, inciting him to take violent action. 'We need to talk, Peta. I need to say what I should have said all those years ago. I want to know what's going on here.'

Outside, footsteps thumped down the hotel corridor. Peta jumped up at the sound of hammering at the door. Harold opened it to admit Mark, followed closely by two paramedics and Williams' three-strong police force.

Chaos ensued as Jaime watched Peta go from numbly answering Mark's questions to a complete quivering mess as shock set in. He couldn't stop the stab of jealousy as Peta went straight into Mark's arms. There was no reason she should seek comfort in his. Mark was the one who had been there for her when he'd abandoned her, when she'd found herself in this crazy, mixed-up mess that had unfolded here tonight. It made perfect sense that she'd turn to her brother.

'Thanks,' said Mark as he showed the paramedics out after they'd tended minor scrapes and bruises and given Peta a sedative. He turned to the three police officers. 'I think we have enough to work with back at the station. Harold, damage control. Can you please make sure the hotel guests and staff are reassured? They need to know they're not in any danger. We need to shut down any rumours, so the press doesn't get wind of it.' Mark held Peta close.

'I'm sure I can come up with a reasonable explanation. The town will close ranks against the media. They look after their own here. I'll organise us a room change while I'm at it. No good being in here with a busted window.'

'Good man. Maybe help Peta to her room before you do while I have a chat to Jaime. We can move her a little later. Peta, why don't you go and have a lie down and let the sedative do its job?'

Wordlessly, she eased out of his arms and walked across the room, her steps weary and her spirit broken, her shoulders slumped in a way that made Jaime want to go after her, to comfort her and tell her he'd take care of everything. As soon as he knew what exactly he was dealing with here.

Mark put a hand on Jaime's arm and shook his head as Jaime made a move to go after her. 'Harold will go with her to make sure she's okay. I have some explaining to do.'

Jaime raised his eyebrows. 'No kidding. For a minute there I thought I was back in the warzone,' he replied, his face drawn in grim lines.

Mark shifted on his feet. 'That's closer to the truth than you think, mate.' He grimaced. 'Would you like another drink?'

Jaime shook his head. 'I have a feeling I'm going to need a clear head. Question and answer time, mate. This is Williams, for God's sake, not the city where crime happens on every corner. The only time anyone has ever used a gun here is for putting an injured horse or cow out of their misery.'

'Things change.' Mark cleared his throat as he sat down. 'Might be best to start at the beginning. Peta had some health problems after you left town.'

'What sort of health problems?'

'A breakdown. For a while she stopped caring, stopped eating. She slowly deteriorated and because her immune system was weak, she contracted pneumonia following a nasty bout of flu,' Mark explained. 'While she was recovering in hospital, she was tracked down by a nightclub owner named Paul Price. He'd heard her sing at the bush dance that year and was keen on promoting her career. We checked him out thoroughly and he came up squeaky clean. Not so much as an unpaid parking ticket. Before we knew it, he'd swept her off her feet and married her. She soared to fame under his guidance and made him some money to get his nightclub, The Golden Diva, off the ground.'

'He screwed her over for money?'

Mark shook his head. 'Peta was very wise there. She made him sign a contract to pay back all the money she'd loaned him to start the nightclub. Her lawyers made sure all her earnings were kept out of his reach. Paul got into gambling and managed to lose almost everything he owned. To get himself out of trouble, he got involved with the wrong sort of people. He let them use the nightclub as a front for money laundering and drug running. Peta became suspicious. He kept trying to get her to sign over her fund management to him as he got deeper and deeper in the shit. She filed for a divorce, and it was pushed through the courts because of some … shall we say, extenuating circumstances.'

'Extenuating circumstances? How much worse did it get?'

Mark shook his head. 'Much worse. Paul liked to use his fists to get what he wanted, and he used them often. She obtained a restraining order against him and began doing some investigating of her own. She managed to get hold of video evidence that would lock him and his friends up for life. She came to me with the story, but before she could hand over the evidence, Price kidnapped her daughter and is using her as a bargaining tool to get it back.'

'Wait. She has a daughter?' Peta was a mum. She'd be good at that. Better if her circumstances were different. He pushed down the jealousy that gnawed for a moment. He'd thrown away his chance at having a family with her. He couldn't begrudge her the baby she'd always wanted.

'A little girl. Bella. She's a sweetheart.' Mark smiled sadly. 'We need to find her. I can't bear to think what might happen if we don't.'

Disgust shuddered through Jaime. A man who threatened the lives of women and children deserved to be locked away. 'But why bring her back to Williams? Do you know where he's holed up?'

'We haven't been able to pinpoint where exactly. He's smart and bloody slippery. We're working on it. Trust me. There are a lot of places to hide here, a lot of abandoned properties that would make the perfect cover. All we need is for him to make a mistake, and he's getting desperate enough to make one.' Mark paused, his fists clenched. 'As for why here ... it's a control thing, and maybe even punishment. She vowed she would never come back here again after you left her. He knew the reason she wanted to get out of town. You've never been Paul's favourite person. She never really got over you, Jaime. No matter how hard she tried.'

Jaime winced as Mark's words hit their target. 'I didn't want to leave her. I had to.'

'But you did, and we can't change that. I'm sorry, you weren't meant to get involved in this mess. All I wanted was for you and my sister to meet face to face and put the past to rest. We have to find Price before it's too late.'

Jaime eyed his friend with dread in his heart. 'Agreed.'

Mark grimaced. 'I think your presence has added fuel to his anger. He's losing control. What happened tonight ups the ante. He's getting desperate.'

Jesus, he couldn't begin to imagine what Peta was going through right now. How was she even holding it together? 'Then we need to stop him. What can I do to help?'

Mark looked at him, his gaze assessing. 'This is your last chance to walk away.'

Jaime thumped his fist into his hand. Paul Price had no intention of letting him walk away unscathed. 'I'm in and there's no way out until we've nailed the bastard. Almost getting my throat cut and getting shot at means I'm as involved as I could possibly get.'

Mark rubbed his hand over his face. 'I always knew you were made of stronger stuff. It's going to be a tough fight. It may take days, or it may take weeks. Hostage situations always do.'

'We're in limbo until the big move to Perth takes place. Mining operations run like a well-oiled machine here at the moment. My people will take care of things if I take some personal time out.'

'His game plan keeps changing,' Mark warned. 'I never thought he'd do anything to harm anyone in this town. Looks like he's crazier than I gave him credit for.'

'I'm not going anywhere until this is over.'

He'd let Peta down before. He'd been handed an opportunity to right his wrongs, one he wished wasn't necessary. What would he have done had that bullet struck home and killed Peta? But if what Mark was saying was true, the bullet might have been meant for him. He shuddered at the thought. It was the least he could do to protect her from this maniac and if that meant helping put Paul Price away for life, he wasn't walking until it was over.

Mark blew out a breath. 'He's taken this to the next level. Once we know for sure what we're up against, I'll fill you in. I think you should stay here tonight. It'll be safest. I can't risk him taking a third shot at you.'

'He wouldn't be the first to. But I get that he won't try again here at the hotel. Too public, too risky.'

'Exactly. Don't let Peta anywhere near the doors or windows. You and Harold can take shifts to keep an eye on her. Once we have a lead on Price, we'll know where we're at. Meanwhile, I'll pick up your gear and drop it off after I've made my report. For now, though, get some sleep. Harold will take the first shift.'

Harold returned to the room at the tail end of his words and scowled at Jaime. 'I've organised another suite. Is it really necessary that pretty boy here stays?'

'Since he has a target painted on his back … yes. Your only concern here tonight is ensuring Peta's safety. The sooner we get this over with the better it is for everyone. We need all the help we can get. So, play nice, boys.'

'I don't play nice with arseholes. I'll start moving our stuff across the hall.'

As Harold turned on his heel and walked away, Mark smiled apologetically at Jaime. 'Harold has a soft spot for Peta,' he explained. 'He was on the emergency response unit when Peta's troubles first began. Before he turned to the hard stuff, Price used to get really drunk and get stuck into Peta. Harold was on duty a few times when he beat up on her, but she wouldn't press charges. If he gets hold of Paul Price before I do, it's highly likely the man won't live to stand trial.'

'I'm right behind him and it's a race as to who gets there first.' Jaime shook his head. 'What about your parents? Why didn't they do something about it?'

'They didn't know. Peta tried hard to keep it from them. Dad was sick with lung cancer. He didn't have long to go. Mum had her hands full taking care of him.'

Mark sighed. 'If he'd done a really bad number on her, she wouldn't go home to visit until the bruises healed. Things got worse after Bella was born. He was extremely jealous of her.'

'Why didn't she leave him?' Jaime asked.

'That's the thing most people don't get. Victims caught up in the cycle of an abusive relationship seldom can leave. For many reasons. Price had some pretty scary buddies. He threatened to use his connections, and he has. I think she also had some misguided feeling that she owed it to him to stay. He rescued her at a pretty bad time in her life.'

'Owed him for what?' Jaime interrupted again.

Mark shrugged. 'That's not my business to tell. She finally decided to seek a divorce when he pulled a knife on her. Twenty stitches later, she decided that she was putting herself and her child at risk if she stayed. The violence was escalating. It took a lot of spunk to make the move. Peta thought she had her security, the evidence against him … until he got desperate. He needed that evidence, so he kidnapped Bella, putting him back in control.'

Jaime buried his head in his hands, suddenly feeling very tired. 'She has been through a nightmare, hasn't she? If only I'd stuck by her, none of this would have happened. The military seemed like a good way to put distance between us, give her room to grow. A lifetime of hell for Peta and it's my fault.'

Mark put a hand on his friend's shoulder. 'It's not your fault, Jaime. This is your chance to build a new relationship. Don't let it start on the ruins of an old one. Life doesn't give many second chances, don't blow it.' He stood. 'I have to get down to the station to put through the report of your run in with Paul and sort out what happened here tonight. Peta won't be happy when she finds you here in the morning. I know she'll kick up a stink when she finds out you're part of the search party. I think I'll leave you to handle that.' He grinned as he strode towards the door. 'Even I'm not that brave.'

Jaime shook his head. If only that was all they had to worry about. 'Coward.'

'Too right, mate. I've copped a few cuffs to the ear over the years I'm sure were meant for you.' Mark walked out the door, locking it behind him.

Jaime shook his head and set off to make peace with Harold. He found him securing the covers around Peta. Harold looked up as Jaime approached the foot of the bed to study Peta as she slept.

'I've moved most of the stuff across the hall. Suite 204. I'm about to move Peta.' He held out a room key and loomed over Jaime, his bulk intimidating to anyone who didn't know he had the heart of a teddy bear. 'You hurt her again, Jaime Caruso, and I'll rip your head off and shove it up your arse. This kid's had more than her fair share of unhappiness and I plan to make sure it doesn't happen again once this ordeal is over.' The big man's voice was a low growl. 'Peta is like family to me. She's been through enough. Don't put her through any more. If you're not planning to stick around for good, get out now.'

Jaime tucked the key into his pants pocket. 'Relax, Harold. I know the score. If I stuff up again, you have my permission to bounce my arse right out of here.'

'Don't tempt me.'

Jaime looked at Peta, her hair splayed across the pillow. Even in sleep she was restless. A frown drew her brows together and dark circles shadowed the skin under her eyes. 'I try not to make the same mistake twice.' He'd spent too many years regretting making it once. 'I'll be careful. You want me to carry her?'

Harold's filthy look said 'no' really clearly.

'Fine. I'll get the door for you.'

Jaime walked out of the room, stepped across the hall and opened the door to Suite 204. He had to prove himself first. He got that. Moving into the suite, he walked into the main bedroom and pulled back the covers, ready for Harold to put Peta to bed.

The big man strode past him and settled her down. She stirred before snuggling back down again without opening her eyes. Rest was the best thing for her. Jaime sighed and went in search of a place to sleep.

Thank God for Harold and Mark who'd been there for Peta when she'd needed them. It could have been a whole lot worse if they weren't. What kind of a man raised his hand to a woman and beat her so badly she ended up in an emergency room? The same kind of man who'd steal a child and use her to get what he wanted. A man he'd like to see dead because jail time would be too easy on him.

He closed the door on the suite and locked it before making himself as comfortable as possible on the sofa. His feet hung over the edge and the cushions were old and soft with a slightly musty smell. Sleep wouldn't come easily tonight, and it wouldn't only be from an uncomfortable, lumpy old sofa. Guilt ate into his mind like acid from a slow feed drip. If he'd had the balls to take what he wanted years ago, Peta's life could have been very different.

Chapter Six

Jaime awoke three hours later to Peta screaming. He leaped up, wincing as his cramped muscles contracted. Ignoring the searing pain, he sprinted to Peta's room. The sheets crumpled beneath her as she tossed about in her sleep, crying out. He put his arm under her neck to lift and cradle her against his shoulder.

'It's okay, baby, you're dreaming. Wake up, Peta,' he said, gently shaking her shoulder. 'Peta, open your eyes.'

Harold burst through the door. 'What the hell? What are you doing, Caruso?'

Jaime looked up at him. Harold had one hand on his holster and a murderous look on his face. 'Easy, tiger. She's having a nightmare. I'm trying to wake her up.'

Harold let his hand drop and moved to the small bathroom. He returned with a glass of water. 'Here.'

Jaime held the cool liquid against her lips and dribbled the water lightly through the narrow opening of her lips. 'Where were you anyway? Aren't you supposed to be on duty?'

'What, a man can't take a piss now? Who put you in charge?'

'You could have woken me to take over. How hard would that have been?'

'It wasn't necessary. Don't tell me how to do my job. Where were you for the last decade, arsehole?'

Jaime bit back a response as the barb hit home.

'Stop it. Stop fighting,' Peta whispered. 'Please.'

Jaime hugged her closer, resting his cheek on her soft, silky head. 'It's okay, honey. We're here. You're safe.'

She looked up at him again, clutching his shirt, the sadness in her eyes so intense he felt his own eyes burn. 'I'm so afraid. He has my little girl, Jaime. I know what he can do.'

'We'll find them, I promise. She'll be fine.' He hoped to God he was right.

'What if we don't?'

Jaime glanced at Harold as he eased her back down onto the pillows. 'We won't give up until we do. You've got the best team on it. Try and get some sleep, honey.'

'Stay with me. Please. I just need you to hold me. Every time I close my eyes …'

Jaime looked at Harold again who shrugged. 'A man's gotta do what a man's gotta do.' Then he walked out.

One point in his favour. He slipped under the covers and, taking her back into his arms, spooned her comfortably against his chest. It felt so good, he thought, so right. It felt like coming home.

Dawn broke through the blinds and Jaime stirred, reluctant to open his eyes in case last night had been another dream. He breathed deeply. Nope, not a dream. He would recognise Peta's perfume anywhere. It still haunted him every night.

Opening his eyes, Jaime allowed his gaze to wander over Peta's sleeping form. She'd turned to face him in the night—the longest night of their lives. Her hand rested at his waist. The cool cotton of her shirt caressed his heated skin. No, not her shirt, his shirt—the one she'd gone home in that last night they'd been together. Well worn—like she wore it often. Gently he rubbed his chin against her hair, picked up the silky strands and let them fall through his fingers. She still used the same shampoo. The smell was so familiar.

Jaime hugged her closer against him for a second before he levered his arm out from beneath her and laid her back against the pillow beside him. She mumbled in protest as her hand slipped from his waist and reached out to rest it on his chest instead. He propped himself up on his arm to look down at her, anchoring her hand against his heart. How badly he wanted to set things straight. But that couldn't happen until her little girl was safe and her mind was at ease again. If he could give her anything in the world, he'd give her that.

A knock at the door and the welcome smell of coffee announced the arrival of Harold. He took in the intimacy of the scene as he held the mug out to Jaime. 'Sedatives make her fuzzy. She hates having to take them. If I were you, I'd get out of here before she wakes up. She's not likely to remember asking you to keep her company.'

The hostility was absent in his tone, but the wariness remained in his narrowed gaze. Jaime met his look with a defiant one of his own and removed the tangled sheet from his waist. Thank God he'd kept his boxer shorts on, or Harold might have cause to hurt him. His body clearly betrayed that Peta still had power over his hormones, and the danger they were in hadn't diluted it.

Harold turned away, but not before Jaime caught the hint of a smile in his eyes. 'Need a cold shower, arsehole?' he asked.

'A joke, Harold? Don't tell me you're lightening up. And what? Arsehole's my name now? Just as well you make good coffee,' he answered with a mock salute of the mug as he made his way out the door.

In the outer room of the suite, Jaime stretched his cramped muscles. He could hear the muffled conversation from the bedroom as Peta awoke. A knock at the door to the suite made him start and almost spill his coffee.

'It's me,' Mark called out through the wood and Jaime crossed over to open the door. 'Special delivery. Your shaving gear.' Mark eyed the stubble on Jaime's jaw. 'And boy, do you need it. Some clean clothes and breakfast.' He held up the gym bag first and then the brown paper bag.

Jaime shook his head. 'Why the hell are you so chirpy so early in the morning?' he asked, pinching the bridge of his nose.

A dull thud beat behind his eyes, and he could only blame it on lack of sleep and too much happening the night before. He wasn't used to being stabbed, shot at or confronted by a past he'd worked so hard to bury. Either way he'd bleed. And holding Peta in his arms again. If only the circumstances could have been different.

Mark popped muffins from the paper bag into the microwave and set the timer. 'Go and shower. You'll feel better for it. Make it quick. Cold muffins taste shit.'

Jaime picked up his kit and headed in the direction of the shower. He soaped himself and washed his hair then allowed the warm water to rinse his body, enjoying the invigorating spray as it battered away the numbness of sleep. Turning the water off, he reached around the curtain for a towel and realised there wasn't one.

'Damn. Mark, bring me a towel please, mate?' A few seconds later the door opened, and he swept the curtain aside. But it wasn't Mark who stood there.

The towel slipped from Peta's hands as she stared at his damp nakedness. 'Oh.' Then surprise and the flicker of heat in her eyes faded to irritation. 'Why are you still here? Didn't I ask you to go?'

Clearly Mark and Harold had been right. She wasn't pleased that he'd stayed. Apparently she didn't remember him holding her close all night either. That shouldn't hurt so much. 'Yes, right before you asked me to stay. Your brother filled me in on a few details and I chose not to go after all.'

'You had no problem leaving before.'

Now that he knew what put the edge on her words, he could let that one go to the keeper. 'Not this time.'

'Then you're a bigger idiot than I thought.' She picked up the towel she'd dropped and shoved it into his hands. 'Mark and Harold went out to get some more milk. Here's your towel.'

Quickly, he wrapped it around his waist because damn it, his body remembered hers even if she didn't remember his. 'Thanks.' The bathroom suddenly seemed even smaller. He had no choice but to stand close in the tiny cubicle, absorbing her body heat. 'You should go.' Before he forgot all the reasons he shouldn't take her in his arms and kiss her like he meant it.

Peta's gaze roamed across the coarse curls plastered damply to his chest before she cleared her throat and looked away, blushing.

Jaime's gaze dropped to her slim, shapely legs bare below the hemline of his shirt. His shirt. Damned if it didn't make his heart sing that she still wore it, never mind kept it all these years. He swallowed as his gaze wandered up, taking in her sleep-tousled hair, her lovely, flushed face. Closing his eyes, he inhaled her essence, his body responding as heat spread through him.

Jaime wanted to hold her so badly, to feel her warmth against him like he had during the night. He groaned inwardly at the mental images his thoughts provoked. His arms ached with restraint as his hands gripped the front of the towel which barely concealed his desire. The need to hold her, kiss her, won as his eyes opened to search her face. He reached out to ease her closer.

'Jaime,' she whispered, searching his face.

He read the uncertainty in her eyes. 'One kiss. Only one. To see if you taste the same as I remember.'

Even as he promised it, he knew it wouldn't be enough. He tugged her against him, his arms going around her to hold her closer, loose enough for her to wiggle out of, yet tight enough to ask her to stay. On tiptoe, she reached for his lips. He met her halfway, his mouth soft on hers, the lightest touch a request for more.

When she whimpered and burrowed closer, the towel the only barrier between them, he gave her more. His mouth played on hers, his tongue teasing as his hand cupped her bottom and he held her closer. Oh Lord, he remembered how good her naked skin felt against his. Her fingers grazed down his side, leaving a trail of fire in their wake, found the towel and tugged to loosen it.

The slamming of the front door made them jump apart. Peta's hand flew to her lips, her cheeks pink, her gaze hot on his.

'Peta? Where are you?'

Jaime's mind snapped to full alert as he heard Mark's footsteps move closer. He grasped the top of the towel with one hand and patted her bottom with the other. 'Your brother's timing sucks as always.'

'I'd say that's not a bad thing.'

'I won't apologise.'

'I didn't ask you to.' She dropped her hands to her side. 'But it won't happen again.'

Damned if she wasn't right, but he didn't need to like it. 'I make no promises.'

Her eyes turned sad. 'You never did.'

And that truth hit him square in the chest and made him feel two feet tall and every inch the arsehole Harold had chosen to identify him by. 'I was an idiot.'

She turned towards the door and her silence said it

all. She didn't have to agree with him. When this madness was over, they'd talk it through, sort it out, maybe stand a second chance.

'Hey, Peta?'

She stopped in the doorway. 'Yeah?'

'Shirt's wet.'

She looked down at her chest imprinted with his shape. 'Damn you, Jaime Caruso.'

There was no anger in her words as she made a dash for her bedroom. Jaime set about the task of shaving. At least now he knew she wasn't immune. Under her cool facade, the flame was still very much alive.

Finishing up, he passed her on her way to the bathroom he'd just vacated. She avoided his eyes as she brushed past him, their bodies touching for a brief, blissful moment. Jaime smiled and reached out his hand to touch her arm.

'It's going to be okay,' he reassured her.

She nodded, but still wouldn't look at him.

He followed the smell of muffins and coffee. Whatever had happened between them just then would have to be dealt with, but it could wait. There were more important matters to deal with right now, like finding her daughter.

Chapter Seven

The three men were seated around the breakfast bar when Peta came out dressed in old denims and a fresh shirt, with a renewed will to fight. They had their heads close together, talking in hushed tones. She heard Paul's name mentioned.

'Whatever you're planning, you'd better let me in on it. What that bastard did last night was the last straw. I'm done playing his games.' And their plan had better include something that ensured her daughter's safety. With Paul's behaviour so erratic, she didn't want anyone taking chances. She bore her own scars from his volatility.

Peta's phone rang, interrupting Mark's response. She'd been expecting it, never doubted for a minute that it would be him. Paul would ring because the narcissist in him needed someone to blame for his actions. All this was her fault. She'd made him do it. Peta breathed deeply before picking it up, tapping the green icon and setting it on speaker phone. She couldn't afford to make him angry. Not while he had Bella.

'Hello, Peta.' The familiar deep voice sent unpleasant shivers down Peta's spine. 'I see your boyfriend's back in town. I really hope I managed to bury at least one shot?'

She resisted the urge to rise to the bait. 'Let me speak to Bella. I need to know she's okay.'

'So that's a no then? What a pity. Shameful waste of a bullet.'

And this was where she played how-to-deal-with-a-narcissist, the game that dogged her life. One she'd had to become good at or feel the pain, physically and emotionally. She closed her eyes. *Kiss up or shut up. Know what you want. Emphasise disappointment.* 'What would people think, Paul? What would they say if they knew you wouldn't let me see her? Mum will be very disappointed by your behaviour.'

Paul laughed, a cruel and bitter sound. 'You only have yourself to blame. I told you no cops and who do I see keeping a close watch? No one other than your two pet guard dogs. I bet you've got me on speaker phone and they're listening in as we speak. I hope you've got each other's backs, pigs, because I'll be looking out for you,' he taunted, like a child playing a game of tag. Then his voice took on a dangerous, threatening pitch that sent chills down Peta's spine. God help her, she knew the consequences of that tone. 'Do you think I'm playing games here? I meant it when I said Bella will die if you don't cooperate, bitch. I told you to stay out of the public eye, but you disobeyed me. You know what that means, don't you?'

Peta didn't need to look at Mark for a cue. She knew this game better than anyone. *Kiss up.* 'I know. I'm really sorry,' she said aloud, 'What can I do to make it up to you?'

Paul snorted. 'Too easy, babe. You don't normally agree that quickly. I used to have to beat it out of you, remember?'

Peta's nerves stretched to breaking point. There were so many things she wanted to shout at him, to put the blame where it belonged for how their marriage had started and ended. *Shut up, don't bite.* 'Just tell me what you want me to do.' *Know what you want.* 'All I want is my daughter back and you out of my life for good.'

Mark tapped her arm and shook a warning finger at her. Getting too sassy with Paul would make things worse. She shook Mark's hand away and glared back at him. Just because she knew how to play the game didn't mean she had to stick to the rules. Reality and the fight to survive had changed that.

Paul's voice came back low and dangerous. 'Watch your mouth, Peta. You know from experience that I don't make idle threats. Go to the old Post Office on

Main Street at ten-thirty tonight and leave the goods in the doorway in the side alley. Take your mobile phone with you and wait for my call. Leave the cops at home. Come alone or you'll never see that bastard's child again. I could so easily have killed him tonight. I should have. Maybe that would have made you obey.'

Peta looked at Mark, eyes wide. He gestured for her to stay calm. Her gaze flicked to Jaime, and she knew he'd picked up on Paul's words. *That bastard's child.* Anger pulled his lips tight and the lines in his cheeks deepened. The furrow on his brow told her he'd heard, processed and understood Paul's insinuation. Jaime stood and took a step closer before Mark waved him back.

Peta spoke again, more calmly this time. 'I'll give you what you want. Please, just don't hurt Bella. For God's sake, Paul, she's an innocent child. Your fight is with me.'

Paul snorted. 'You don't get it, do you, bitch? You would if you thought about it hard enough. I looked after you and your daughter while you hankered for him. For years I played second fiddle to a lousy memory while I boosted your career and fed you. Yet you couldn't even help me out when I was in trouble.'

And then she broke the most important rule of the game — *don't* — and argued back. 'The trouble was of your own making, Paul. I wasn't about to let you gamble away my daughter's inheritance, or waste it on bloody drugs,' Peta yelled, slapping off Mark's warning hand and pushing him away.

'Just be there with the parcel. And the evidence better all be there, or you'll never see your daughter alive again.'

Anger, despair and fear raced through her chased by frustration, as she stabbed at the red icon to end the call. Oh, dear God, what had she done? Years of playing the game and she'd let her emotions rule. When would she learn? If he hurt Bella now, it would be her fault.

Harold wrapped her in a bear hug and held her until she'd calmed down. 'You've got to stop having a go at him, love. It won't help making him angrier,' he said.

She sobbed into his shirt. 'I know. I didn't mean to. I just want this nightmare over. If he hurts her, I swear to God when I find him —'

'We will find her, Peta. We'll play back that call through the analysing app and see what we can pick up in background noise. Anything that helps us pinpoint his position.'

She had to believe they would. Peta nodded, hugging Harold tightly before handing him her phone. She moved away and took the mug of coffee Jaime held out to her, couldn't meet his eyes because she knew she'd see anger there too. Mark was right. She should have told him about Bella earlier. He didn't deserve to find out this way.

Mark picked up his keys. 'We'll take this down to

the station and play it back to the guys. They might recognise something we don't. You two need to talk. Just so you know, Jaime, I'm only leaving her in your care because I know you have the training for it to keep her safe.'

'Stay away from the doors and windows,' added Harold with a pat to Jaime's shoulder. 'Take it easy, Caruso.'

Peta pulled her lips tight. Easy wasn't the word she'd use for the emotions he'd be feeling right now. God knew, she'd felt them all when she'd found out about her baby. Shock, anger, regret, dread, and finally an uneasy acceptance filled with concern for the future. And then when Bella was born, an overwhelming love for the tiny little life she'd held in her arms and commitment to giving her the best of everything she could. She'd failed. Completely.

As the door closed behind Mark and Harold, she wiped the tears away with the back of her hand and let anger replace them. If she stayed angry — at herself, at Jaime, at Paul — she'd stay fighting for her daughter's return because giving up and crawling into a hole of despair wasn't a choice.

Peta pushed past Jaime to the kitchen, her arm brushing his as she passed. He stood silent, as solid as the granite face of Wave Rock without the curve to its back, and equally as cold.

At the sink, she let the water run hot, added the

dishwashing liquid. Going through the motions. It's all she seemed to do these days. She piled the dishes into the water, determined to keep her hands busy as her mind churned and her desperation grew. She scrubbed vigorously at the plates, slamming them onto the rack to dry.

Jaime remained unmovable in the centre of the room. She felt his eyes on her back as she fought her inner battle and silently dared him to challenge her on what he'd heard. Instead, he stood watching her, his own anger simmering. He'd want answers, ones she wasn't ready to give but was forced to because she hadn't had the good sense to take Bella and run.

'Damn you, Jaime Caruso! Why did you have to show up again?' She turned with an angry growl and threw the wet sponge at him as hard as she could, satisfied as a wet spot bloomed squarely in the middle of his chest.

Peta turned back to the sink and stared at the bubbles. Maybe living with a narcissist had made her into one because, God damn it, she needed someone else to blame. None of this would have happened if Jaime hadn't walked out on her all those years ago. Even as she thought it, she knew she was wrong, but the anger and despair wouldn't stop growing. The whole situation had spiralled out of control so quickly, and she had no way to stop it.

Chapter Eight

Jaime stared at the foam dripping down the front of his shirt and transferred his gaze to the tense stretch of Peta's shoulders. His own anger had morphed into disbelief. He had a child. Bella was his daughter. And he might never get to see her alive.

He'd seen horror unfold when war intervened and tore children from their parents' arms. He'd lived through the despair of death and separation. He'd never wanted to live through it again, not when it involved his own family. One he didn't know he had. But being angry with Peta wouldn't solve anything. If only she'd told him about the baby.

He bent and picked up the sponge from the puddle on the floor, walked across to the sink, reached around her and dropped it back into the water with the splash.

Peta pulled out the drain plug and shook the water from it. 'You picked a bloody good time to come back, didn't you? What really happened all those years ago? And don't you dare feed me all that rubbish about giving me my space and letting me grow up. There was something or someone behind your decision, wasn't there?' She turned to face him squarely, her body taut with anger. 'I loved you, damn it.'

Fine, so they'd deal with the past first. Jaime's hands itched to reach for her tense shoulders, pull her into his arms and hold her tightly against him. Because when he did, it made explanations easier, gave him the anchor he needed. But holding her would be a mistake.

He took a small step away from her and leaned a hip against the counter top. In this frame of mind, she was more likely to fight him if he tried, and he'd prefer she came into his arms willingly, like she had earlier when the lightest touch of her lips to his made him remember how good it had been. Why had she kept this secret from him? Why hadn't she come to him when she was in trouble? He pressed his lips together. He hadn't exactly made it easy for her leaving the way he had.

He picked up a cloth from its resting place, contemplated drying the dishes and then tossed it impatiently back onto the rack. They could wait. What he'd heard coming out of Paul Price's mouth couldn't. And there was no point delaying the truth any longer.

He watched as she struggled to gain composure and force the anger to drain away.

'Let's sit down and I'll try to explain.' He gestured towards the chairs at the kitchen bench. 'I came to do some explaining last night, but things got a little out of hand.' Jaime grimaced as she followed him and settled onto a chair.

He reached for her hand, a little surprised when she didn't resist or pull away. Maybe she needed an anchor too. He rubbed her long fingers with his, loving the soft feel of them. Remembering how they'd felt against his skin all those years ago. She had a right to know the truth. Just as he deserved the same from her.

'My parents were putting pressure on me to end it with you. Dad had it in his head that Maria Ferraro would make the perfect marriage partner for me. She was older, more settled, groomed to be an executive's wife and ready to be imported from Italy on the offer of a wedding ring.' His lips pulled tight. 'Not my idea of the perfect relationship. You, on the other hand, were so innocent, so full of energy and dreams. If I tied you down then, I would have stomped all over that, Peta.'

'You at least could have talked to me about it instead of deciding my future for me.'

He winced. Hindsight had always been a brilliant teacher. He'd ignored the fact that Peta was wise beyond her years, even back then. 'I had a reputation for being disastrous at long-term relationships. Until I met you.'

When he'd been tempted to believe he could do commitment after all. 'I didn't want to hurt you, Peta. Even I knew serious relationships that started so young could create bitter voids between two people down the track. I didn't want that to happen to us. My mother was convinced you were too young and too impressionable to make a choice. Dad wanted me to concentrate on learning to run the business. Having a young wife would be a distraction. They didn't think you could handle the pressure or the amount of time I'd spend away from home on business.'

Peta frowned. 'And you didn't think you could discuss this with me?'

'You were nineteen. You were so young.'

'Too young to know what I wanted? How dare you claim to know what I wanted or needed.' Anger coloured her cheeks and those beautiful eyes that haunted his dreams flashed green fire. 'I don't remember being too young for you to take me to bed.'

Bitterness twisted through her words making him flinch. 'I wanted to marry you, Peta, but not right away. Dad wanted me to take on the shareholder portfolio. I would be away off-shore more than I would be home. How could I ask a nineteen-year-old with her whole future ahead of her to wait for me while I travelled around the world, while my parents planned my wedding to someone else behind my back? So, I decided to give you your freedom. And then I took mine because

I couldn't face having you so close and not being able to reach for you.'

'So, you joined the military? Put yourself in the middle of a war you may never have survived?'

'I had something tangible to fight for. A cause, freedom and limited free time to think about what could have been. Even when I was granted leave, I stayed because I had nothing to come back for. By the time I came to terms with what I really wanted, I was in too deep to leave, and you were all over the front page of magazines and newspapers, happily married with a successful career.' He looked down at their hands. 'I'm sorry, Peta. I honestly thought it was for the best. I loved you too much to let you tie yourself down to someone who couldn't commit. I had to learn to do that first.'

'And you committed yourself to a war you didn't have to fight to prove that?' Peta raised her hand to his face, her palm warm against his skin. 'I loved you, Jaime. What about what I wanted, what I felt? You didn't even ask me. You just went ahead and decided for both of us.'

'Arrogance, stupidity … name it, I lived it. Then I closed my heart and mind and fought a war because thinking of you happy with someone else drove me insane. Knowing you weren't breaks my heart.'

'Maybe you were right. Maybe I was too young.' Peta sighed as she dropped her hand away. 'I hated you for a long time after you left. My life was just beginning to have meaning and then you dropped out of it. So did the bottom of my world. I was ill when I met Paul. He helped me at a time when I needed support and promised me a career to keep me occupied. He came through for me. When Bella was born, I had someone to love again. That was probably the beginning of Paul's problems. I put so much time and love into Bella that at times I forgot he existed. And now Bella's gone,' she said, her voice sad, the words quivering on her tongue.

Jaime lifted her off the chair and held her close, his heart aching for Peta and the daughter he had yet to meet. He had so much lost time to make up for. 'We will find her. I promise.'

'You made promises in the past and couldn't keep them. Why should I believe it will be any different this time,' she asked, her voice muffled against his shoulder.

'Because I mean it. Trust me again. I know that's a lot to ask right now, but please trust me. Do you believe in second chances?' he asked, lifting her face to his.

She looked up at him, her lips so tempting just below his. All he needed to do to taste them was inch closer.

'I do, but I can only cope with one thing at a time. Let me find my daughter first.'

Jaime kissed the top of her head instead. 'Agreed,' he answered and lifted her back onto the chair, ignoring the demands of his body. 'Why didn't you tell me about Bella?'

How much would she tell him, and would it be the truth? There was no mistaking the meaning behind the words Paul Price had tossed into the ring or the vindictiveness behind them. It must have driven the man nuts to know he was raising another man's child when he was so clearly obsessed with Peta.

'How soon after I left did you find out?' he prompted, when she remained silent.

Peta avoided his gaze as he let it skim over face. 'About six weeks later.'

'That last night down by the river.' He'd been desperate and torn, and totally irresponsible in protecting her because all that had consumed his mind was that he'd have to leave her.

'Yes.' She picked up her handbag on the bench top and pulled a well-worn photograph from her purse, taken when Bella was a toddler. 'I have no regrets about that.'

Jaime studied the photo. Dark brown curls danced around a cherub face, big green eyes twinkled as the little girl posed for the picture. If he'd needed proof, it was there in his hands. The Caruso genes were strong, but her eyes were exactly like her mum's.

'She's beautiful.' He tried and failed to keep the regret out of his voice. He'd missed so much of her life. Her first steps, her first day at school, her first Christmas.

'Yes, she is. It's her tenth birthday in a couple of

months,' she choked out. 'I hope … I want to have her home safely before then.'

He wanted that too. Now more than ever. And he hoped Peta would let him be part of his daughter's life. Things could have been so different if he'd only listened to his heart instead of his mind. 'Do you have any more photographs?'

She shook her head. 'Not with me right now.'

Surreal. The enormity of it slammed into his gut. He was a father. Had been one for almost ten years. To a daughter he'd never seen and maybe never would because that little girl was in the hands of a madman. God help Paul Price if he harmed her in any way. 'Why didn't you tell me?'

Peta shifted on her chair, catching her bottom lip between her teeth then releasing it. 'Would it have made a difference to your decision or your family's?'

His eyes snapped to hers, anger rising in his gut. 'Did you think it wouldn't? Good God, Peta, you know me better than that. I could have at least made sure you and the baby were taken care of financially.'

Peta snatched the photo from his hands and put it back in her purse, her spine ramrod straight, ice dripping from her words. 'It wasn't your money I wanted. I was — and still am — quite capable of taking care of my daughter financially.'

'Yes, and by keeping your mouth shut, you've endangered her life and your own.'

Jaime regretted the words the moment they left his tongue. Peta flinched as the shutters descended in her eyes and she retreated inside the shell she wore like armour. What the hell was he thinking laying the blame on her? She'd be feeling guilty enough. He'd been the one to close the door on their relationship, placing her in a position where she couldn't approach him about the pregnancy. He'd made it final.

'I'm sorry. That was unfair and a lousy thing to say.' He ran a hand through his hair, the other on his hip.

'I did what I could, Jaime. If I could change anything in my life at all, it would be that I wasn't strong enough to walk away from him the day he stepped into my hospital room. He was caring, charming and oh so believable in his concern for me. He promised me a dream I could hold on to, something to live for. And when I realised I was being used for his own gain, it was harder to get out than it should have been.'

Her mouth pulled so tight he wanted to ease the crease away with his thumb. He jammed his hands into his pockets. He wanted to reach for her and hold her, ease some of her pain, but her arms hugged her waist in a barrier between them, so he did the only thing he could and listened.

'It didn't take long to reveal his narcissistic side. Add drugs, alcohol and bad company into the mix and he bordered on bi-polar, swinging between mania and deep depression.' Peta raised her eyes to his. 'You have no idea what it's like knowing you'd be hurt if you stayed or dead if you left, because I had no doubt he'd carry out his threats. And if I'd known he'd extend those threats to my daughter, I would have taken the risk and ran. But I didn't.'

Jesus. The thought of what she'd been through made him want to kill Paul Price himself. 'But Mark —'

'Did as much as the law allowed him to in order to protect me without ending up in prison himself or being thrown off the force for it.'

And he'd done nothing except get on with his life and try to forget her.

The door opened as Mark and Harold returned. 'We didn't have much luck with the analytics.' Mark dropped the room key on the table and took in the tension in the room. 'No background noise, nothing to identify his whereabouts.' He watched as Harold bent to wipe up the soapy puddle on the floor near the kitchen sink then looked at Peta and Jaime curiously, catching sight of the still damp patch on Jaime's chest. 'World War Three or just a minor disagreement?' When they both glared at him, he continued, 'Okay, then … on to the plans for tonight. Since Paul's violence has escalated, we're looking at putting a substitute in Peta's place for the drop off —'

Peta dug her heels in. 'No, I go or the deal's off. He's not playing games anymore and I won't do anything that might make him angry enough to take it out on Bella.'

Mark tried to be the voice of reason. 'Peta, he's unstable. Who knows what he's likely to do? The drop off could be a trap. It's too risky. He knows there's no way we're letting you go in there on your own. He'll be ready and waiting for us … and you.'

Peta looked at them, chin raised, her stubborn expression leaving them in no doubt she wasn't in the mood to obey. 'All the more reason why I should be doing what he says. I won't put anyone else's life in danger. There are already too many innocent people involved. It's my daughter's life at stake here. I go tonight and there'll be no argument.' She held up her hand as Mark began to protest. 'If Paul sees you or anyone else show up, he's more likely to harm Bella. You know how hostage negotiation works, Mark. It's me he wants. I know how to handle him. It's been a week since he snatched her. I want her back.'

Mark sighed. 'I had to try. Okay, but be careful and wait for instructions.'

'Surely there's another way?' Jaime shifted on his feet, the thought of Peta walking into danger sending chills up his spine.

'I'll do what I have to do,' she insisted.

Mark glowered. 'You'll do what I tell you to do.'

Her chin rose higher. Jaime admired Peta's strength, even while his heart pounded with fear for her. She'd come a long way since they'd been apart. The naïve young girl he'd left behind was gone for good. No way was she letting anyone do battle on her behalf. In different circumstances it would be as sexy as hell. Right now, it was downright damn scary.

'So, what's the plan then?' Jaime asked, not entirely sure he really wanted to know. There was so much at stake, so much to lose, so many things that could go wrong. No one knew that better than him.

Chapter Nine

Time dragged by as day turned to night and the clock on the kitchen wall marched slowly towards the deadline. Peta's teeth worried her lower lip as images of her daughter flashed through her mind. God help Paul if he'd hurt her in any way. She was so tired of making excuses for him. He'd only harmed himself when he'd refused to seek help with his gambling and drug addiction. Instead, Paul had sunk deeper into the dark underworld of crime. She should have just given him the money.

I helped you earn it. If it wasn't for me you'd still be a nobody.

To him, she was the meal ticket to get exactly what he wanted. Power, wealth and the best drugs money could buy. The man she'd once thought sensitive and caring had become her worst enemy and a bully.

'It's time.' Mark's voice fell into the silence like rocks on a pond.

Peta drew the brown envelope towards her, terror eating at her stomach. What if their plan went wrong? Harold had a copy of the video footage that would lead to an investigation to put Paul and his cronies behind bars for a long time. They had their evidence, now all they needed was to ensure Bella's safety before Mark could make his arrest.

'Let's do this.' Mark placed a mobile phone in Peta's hand. 'Your number, but it has a tracking app enabled which will activate when you receive Paul's call. We'll be following closely and will be within shouting distance at the drop off point. Your wire will pick up any conversation.'

'I'm not happy about the wire.' Paul would know.

'It stays in place, or I pull you out and find a substitute.'

Every second counted. She couldn't afford to argue. 'Let's do this,' she said, apprehension thick in her voice.

'Jaime, keep your distance when this goes down. Don't pull any heroic moves. You're a sitting duck Price is more than happy to shoot at. And I'm fairly sure he won't hesitate to take us down with you,' Mark instructed.

'You're forgetting this shit used to be my day job. I know what to do,' Jaime snapped back.

Mark patted his shoulder as he turned his attention

to the three policemen who made up the Williams police force. They'd been over the plan many times, but there could be no doubt on this mission. So much could go wrong. She didn't want to think about the consequences if it did. While Mark barked out last minute orders and all attention was on him, she slipped her 9mm Beretta Nano from her handbag into her coat pocket.

Main Street was completely deserted as Peta pulled the rental car into the parking lot in front of the Post Office. She scanned the darkened area carefully while touching her coat pocket to reassure herself the gun was close at hand. She would not hesitate to shoot Paul where he stood. If he made even the smallest attempt to hurt her or if he'd harmed so much as a hair on Bella's head, she would pull the trigger with no regrets in the name of self — defence. And then scour every inch of the town in search of her child.

She got out of the car, the brown envelope containing the evidence Paul was so desperate to get heavy in her hands. Fear trickled through her, but she pushed it back. *Kiss up, shut up, know what you want.* The mantra played in her head as she looked around her. There was no sign of the others, but she knew they were there. Paul would too.

'Well, here goes,' she muttered into the microphone concealed in the front of her shirt.

Mark's voice was reassuring in her ear. 'Good girl. Keep your eyes open and don't take any risks. I mean it, Peta.'

'Yes,' she hissed. 'I know how to play.'

'And watch that temper, girl,' he growled. 'Don't antagonise him.'

She didn't bother to respond to that and instead walked down the side of the building and into the alley. She found the darkened doorway and checked her watch. Dead on time. Peta propped the envelope up against the door frame and hurried back to the safety of the car, locking the doors. She could almost feel his evil presence in the creepy, deserted alleyway. She jumped as her mobile phone rang, splitting the silence. Her finger trembled as she pressed the answer button.

'There was no need to run away like that,' Paul's voice taunted. 'You know I won't hurt you, not when you've been such a good girl.' His nasty laugh jarred in her ear, sending frissons of ice-cold fear down her spine. *Play the game*.

'Where is she, Paul? I've given you what you want.' Peta heard the rip of paper as he opened the envelope.

'Well, well … it's all here,' said Paul. 'I didn't think you'd do it, princess.'

'I'm not your princess. You have your evidence. Please give me what I want now.' She struggled to keep her tone even, to keep the impatience and desperation out of it.

'Oh, come on now. Did you really think I'd believe that you and your cop mates would make it this easy? You've never been very co-operative, Peta. You always were too stupid to know when to give me what I needed.' He laughed again, that cruel, taunting sound that made the fine hair on her arms rise with the goosebumps on her skin. 'What did you expect, my dear? That I would take the envelope and just hand her over nicely?'

'Paul, I swear to God, if you don't tell me where Bella is, I am going to get out of this car, hunt you down and kill you myself.'

Peta tried and failed to hold onto her calm. Long, sleepless nights filled with the fear of the unknown took their toll. The vision of her daughter being taken from school. What had Paul said or done to make her go with him so easily? Bella had always been so wary of him.

The soles of her feet still ached from racing out of the school grounds, desperate to find his car still there or discover it was some kind of cruel joke. The awful, tearing pain that had gripped her as she'd seen his car disappear from sight and known it to be true, taking with it what was left of her heart.

'Back off, Peta.' Mark's low growl sounded in her left ear.

'Okay, okay.' Paul's voice echoed in her right. 'We're going to play a little game, a treasure hunt, if you will. Go to the abandoned storage warehouse on Smith

Street. Your next clue is there. I'll be in touch when you get there.'

'I'm done playing games, Paul. You have what you want, now I want my daughter back.'

'I don't have everything I want yet, so you have no choice. Clock's ticking.' The line went silent as Paul hung up.

'Sonofabitch!' she yelled, as she stabbed the button to end the call.

'Take it easy, Peta, or I pull you in,' said Mark in her ear.

She drew in a deep breath and let it go slowly. 'I'm okay, sorry.'

'You're doing fine. He'll hang back a while to see if you're followed so we're going to wait here a while. I've got two people on their way to the warehouse. They'll cover you until we get there,' Mark instructed.

Peta started the engine, put the car in gear and pulled away. As she headed towards Smith Street, she spotted the familiar heavy shape of Paul's imported sedan in her rear-view mirror. The cocky bastard flashed his lights behind her before veering off into a side street. She listened to the squeal of his tyres as he sped away in the opposite direction.

'He's not following me. Why?'

'This is just another clue, all part of his game,' Mark answered. 'Play along, keep your cool. We can't move too quickly on this. He's too volatile.'

'Yeah, yeah, I know.' Peta felt for the gun concealed in her coat pocket, closing her eyes at the comfort of having the cold steel against her palm. 'I'm turning into Smith Street now. The warehouse is dead ahead. There's no sign of Paul.'

'He may have come in from another direction, but my guys would've spotted him. Since they haven't reported any movement except yours, I'm guessing he's on his way to the next rendezvous point,' Mark said. 'We're right behind you now. Wait in the car.'

'I'm not waiting in the car.' She braked outside the warehouse and got out. 'If he's coming for me, I want to meet him face to face, not be taken by surprise.' Because if he did, she wouldn't have time to defend herself. She'd been caught off guard too many times in the past.

'Damn it, Peta, don't do anything stupid,' Mark yelled in her ear, his patience clearly slipping its tether.

'You forget I've played his games before. I know how his sick mind works and I'm damned if I'm going to sit here waiting for him to kill me,' she bit back.

Silent and swift through the darkness, Mark, Harold and Jaime were at her back before she reached for the door handle. Jaime's hand closed around her upper arm as he pulled her towards him, allowing Mark and Harold to take their places in front of the door. They swung it wide, guns aimed into the semi — darkness, the only light coming from the full moon as it filtered through the dusty windows.

'Clear,' Mark called, moving into the building.

Peta's heart sank as Mark and Harold searched every dark, damp corner of the warehouse, knowing they'd find it deserted. A chair stood in the centre of the room, an empty reminder of the horror that might have taken place there on the cold concrete floor.

Peta walked towards it. Thick, coarse rope taunted her from the backrest, sliced through and left to hang loosely from the wooden sides. The cut was clean and sure, typical of Paul's skill with a knife. She'd seen the flash of that blade often enough to recognise its signature cut.

The bastard had tied up her daughter. God knows what else he'd done to terrorise her. Her gaze fell on Bella's blue ribbon where it lay next to the chair. Picking it up, she wrapped it around her fingers and bit down on the nausea that rose to burn in her throat. Her fear turned to frustration. She swallowed around the scream that fought its way to the surface, counting to ten and breathing to stem the anger that took its place.

Jaime turned her to face him, his hands firm yet comforting on her shoulders. 'Peta.' Tipping up her chin, he forced her to meet his gaze. 'Where would he think to go next?'

Peta tried frantically to clear her head. She scrubbed her cheeks with her fists to dry the angry tears. Jaime held her closer, and she laid her head against his warm, comforting chest, closed her eyes to the press of his lips against her forehead.

'Think, Peta. What would his next step be?'

She moved out of his arms. He was too close, she couldn't think, even though the temptation to stay in the comfort of his hold was high. Paul's nature was to plan perfectly. His determination to be smarter, better, above everyone else meant he'd have planned every move right down to the finest detail.

'He said there'd be another clue,' she said. Her eyes dropped to the thin strip of blue wrapped around her fingers. 'The ribbon. Paul bought Bella a blue ribbon at the church fair for her first birthday. We were in London, Trafalgar Square at St Martin's in the Field. The church.' Triumph warred with fear for her daughter. At least they were one step closer. 'That's where we need to go next.'

Her mobile phone rang, a shrill sound that shattered the air around them. Impatiently she hit the answer button. 'I know where you are, Paul. I'm on my way.' *Know what you want.* 'I want to know that Bella is okay. Let me talk to her.' *Kiss up.* 'Please?'

Paul's laugh held no humour. 'You always thought you were smarter than me. Well come on then and bring your playmates with you. I know they're there. I'm in the mood for a good fight. It would be a pity if Bella got hurt though, wouldn't it? I've done such a good job taking care of her up until now.'

Peta closed her eyes. Thank God. Whether he wanted to or not he'd let her know she was okay. 'Paul, I'll warn you again. If you harm Bella in any way, I'll kill you myself. It would be worth the jail time,' Peta said, putting her hand in her coat pocket and closing her fingers around the butt of the gun.

Mark held a warning finger under her nose. 'Stop baiting him.'

Peta pulled her hand out of her pocket and pushed his away. 'I'm on my way.'

'I'll be waiting right here with your bastard child,' Paul replied, and the line went dead.

Abandoning the rental, Peta got into the backseat of Mark's car with Jaime. He slipped his arm across her shoulders and pulled her in for a quick, comforting hug. 'Please be careful in there,' Jaime said.

'I will do what I have to do to get my daughter back safely.'

'Our daughter.'

She couldn't deny that, not now he knew the truth. Peta let her hand come to rest on his thigh. 'Yes, our daughter. But when I find her, I won't give her up again. You need to know that.'

She'd fight with every last breath if he or his family even considered suing for custody. A fact she had to think about, because while he was all nice about it now, things could change in an instant. Just as they had with Paul. Just as they had when Jaime had left.

Under her palm, Jaime's muscles rippled as he shifted on the seat. For one crazy moment, Peta wished they were alone. She wished he'd drag her onto his lap and kiss her senseless until she had no thought in her head except for him. To make the horror go away so she could believe in happiness again. To make her feel the way she used to when they were young and innocent, and monsters like Paul Price didn't exist.

Instead, his hug tightened for a brief moment before he let her go. 'I understand.'

Peta caught Mark's glance in the rear-view mirror and saw the grim set of his features. Next to him, Harold scowled and muttered under his breath. None of them were thinking beyond the next five minutes.

Peta's mobile phone rang. She had no need to check the caller ID and her desire for playing the game was waning. 'Get to the point, Paul. Your little game is starting to piss me off. I've given you what you want, now I want what's mine.'

'Now, Peta, be nice,' Paul said snidely. 'First you have to confess your sins. It's the only way you'll be rewarded. When you get here, leave your henchmen outside. The only one allowed inside is Jaime Caruso. We have a few things to say to each other.'

'You have nothing to say to him. Give me my daughter back and I'll drop any charges against you.'

'I've waited for this moment far too long to let it go, Peta. I think he'll be very interested in what I have to say. I've kept your dirty secret for long enough.'

She was no longer afraid of Jaime's reaction, but if she told Paul that Jaime already knew about Bella, it might send him over the edge. Paul liked power. And knowledge was power. 'He won't care. He never did.' *Rule number four: don't give them the power over you they want.*

'Do as I say, Peta,' Paul ordered. 'Just the two of you or your daughter dies.'

Silence reverberated through the cabin of the car. Fear knotted in Peta's stomach. Had she pushed too far?

As Peta related the instructions from Paul, Mark caught her eye in the rear-view mirror. His were full of warning. She remembered she hadn't had time to tell Mark that Jaime had figured it out already. She stared back at him, resigned to the fact her secret was out.

'He knows, Mark.'

'About time the truth came out,' Mark muttered. 'The timing sucks. We'll talk about it later. Right now, we need to nail this bastard.'

Peta shivered. Even though Jaime knew about Bella now, they could never have a future together. No point in bringing him into their lives if they couldn't be a real family. And the last thing she wanted them to be was a burden.

'You're wrong. I do care.' Jaime's hand covered hers on his thigh.

Peta absorbed the warmth and strength of his touch. She'd need it, enjoy it for the short while she had it because tomorrow came with no guarantees.

'Right,' said Mark, as he swung in through the churchyard gates. 'We'll do as he says. We'll remain outside while you two go in then we'll make our way around to the rear and enter through the vestry to cover you. I won't make a move on him until I know Bella is safe. But if either of you are in danger, I'm taking the bastard down.'

Peta nodded and chewed nervously on her lip as they got out of the car and approached the old church. An array of multi-coloured roses bloomed in the front garden. In the daylight they formed a contrast between the rainbow blooms and the dark red dust, a symbol of life in the desert. In the dark they were yet another ominous shadow hiding a darker evil. Please God, let Bella be in there.

Jaime and Peta approached the old, carved Jarrah doors of the church. In a town as small as Williams, the church doors were closed but never locked. On any other day, the church was a place you came to find peace. Peta hated that today it was anything but a haven. Jaime's hand tightened on hers.

'Let's do this,' he said, encouragingly. 'I won't leave your side until it's over.'

Peta squeezed his fingers in return. 'Thank you.'

Together they pushed open the doors and made their way down towards the pulpit.

'I'm here, Paul,' she called. 'Bring me my daughter.' Desperately she tried to keep her voice normal. 'Paul?' she called again.

'No need to shout, I'm not dead and this is a church. Show some respect please.' Paul's voice came from one of the pews in a darkened corner of the church, his tone mocking. 'So, the dove has returned to the coop.' He walked out of the shadows and onto the red-carpeted aisle. 'And, Jaime, I wish I could say it's nice to meet you at last. Quite the tough guy, aren't you? A knife wound doesn't stop you and you survived that shot without a scrape, I see. Pity that. I might have to work on my aim.'

'Cut to the chase, Paul. Where's my daughter?' Peta said, taking a step forward.

Jaime immediately tugged her back. 'Take it easy,' he whispered.

Peta kept her eyes steady on Paul. In the days they'd been together, she'd learned to read his reactions from his facial expressions. It was dark inside the church, casting shadows across his face. In this lack of light, he was impossible to read. Panic rose in her throat. What if it all went wrong?

'Patience was never your strong point, was it, my little dove?' Through the uneasy silence in the church,

Paul's voice crooned eerily, his words grating down her spine with every syllable, sending goosebumps rippling along her skin, each one containing a veiled threat. She knew the cost of impatience, had paid the price at his hand many times.

Kiss up. 'Come on, Paul. I've done everything you've asked me to do. You've got what you want. Please, let Bella go now,' she said, her hand seeking the gun in her pocket again.

Paul spotted the movement and stepped back, his eyes narrowing. 'Do you really think I believe you have, Peta? Playing games now places both you and your daughter in a very dangerous position.'

Peta sucked in her breath. He stepped closer, his face dark and threatening in the flickering candlelight from the altar. Her movement had triggered the warning bells in his mind, and she knew what that meant. He'd turn on her at any moment. She watched him advance, her heart in her mouth.

'Yes, you've been far too co-operative so far. That's so unlike you,' he mused, 'which means that your friends are out there with their trigger fingers itching to put a hole in my head. Why can't you simply obey instructions?'

Mark and Harold must surely be in the church by now. Please God, don't let them leave it too late. Peta's thoughts raced through her mind. Harold wouldn't need much of an excuse to shoot when it came to Paul.

'We're in, Peta. Ease up. He's tetchy,' Harold whispered into his microphone.

'No more games, Paul.' Peta's voice echoed through the empty church, fear a bitter taste in her mouth driving her to ignore Harold's warning. 'You asked for Jaime and here he is. You have the evidence, which is what you wanted. Give me my daughter. We're done.'

'No,' shouted Paul. 'Do you think I don't know this is a trap? I'm not stupid. Your brother is one of the most decorated cops in the country. They'll nail me as soon as I give you Bella.' He laughed, a cruel and taunting sound that made her belly curl. 'Well, you can't have your daughter now. Not until I'm safely out of the country. Tell me, Peta, does Jaime know the truth about his slutty little girlfriend?' Paul looked from Peta to Jaime and smirked as he played his trump card. 'Do you hear that, Caruso? She's been keeping something very precious from you. You have a daughter. A closely guarded, dirty little secret I raised for you. Pretty little thing. Wouldn't it be awful if she wasn't so pretty anymore?'

Peta's heart missed a beat as Jaime stepped forward with his fists clenched, back straight and temper in full flight. 'You bastard. You don't get to call her names.'

Peta tugged at his sleeve, drawing him back. 'Jaime, don't. Paul, you're wasting time. He already knows about Bella. He knows we have a child together.' Her fingers clenched and unclenched at her side.

Paul's eyes narrowed on her hand. 'What's in your pocket, Peta?'

He lurched forward and grabbed her, hauling her up the aisle away from Jaime. He shook her hard as he raised his fist. She knew how it would feel when he smashed it into her jaw. She'd felt it before. Out the corner of her eye, she saw Jaime run forward.

'No, Jaime, stay there,' she shouted as she blocked the blow before it connected. 'Listen to me, Paul,' she demanded. 'Give me my daughter and I'll give you what you want. A plane ticket, the private jet, whatever you need to get out of my life.'

Paul was in no mood to bargain. He grabbed her wrists and spun her around so that she shielded his body. 'No,' he shouted. 'You will pay for what you've put me through, Miss High-and-Mighty.'

He pinned her hands behind her back. Holding them with one hand, he used the other to pull a knife from his boot and hold it to her throat. Fear overcame reasoning, and all the game rules slipped from her mind as the threat of death rolled in over them. If he killed them now, he'd own her daughter because he'd make sure no one ever found her.

Jaime called out, 'Peta!'

'Move in,' Mark ordered over the wire.

Mark and Harold raced up the aisle behind Paul. He flung Peta aside and ran towards the door, shouldering Jaime in the chest as he attempted to stop him.

Peta pulled the gun out of her pocket and aimed at Paul's departing figure. The bullet skimmed past his calf. 'You bitch. You'll die for this.' He lurched out of the church, down the steps and into the black night.

'Let him go,' Mark yelled at Harold as he made to go after him. 'We still don't know where he's hiding Bella. If we take him down now, he won't tell, and it might take us months to find her.'

Chapter Ten

Adrenaline thumping through her, Peta ran to Jaime. He'd hit his head on the pew going down. He sat on the carpet, feeling out the area on the back of his head with his fingers. Oh God, this was so out of control. Paul had gone beyond the level of his usual maniacal decline which meant his instability balanced on a razor's edge. And the physical strength he'd required to knock someone as solid as Jaime down was typical of a dangerous high. Had she just signed her daughter's death warrant?

'You okay?' Peta knelt beside him. Her heart pounded and her stomach churned.

'Yes,' he hissed. 'Hard head. Did he hurt you?' He searched her face for signs that Paul had landed the threatened punch.

'No.' She touched her forehead to his and closed her

eyes, struggling to keep the tears at bay. 'I'm so sorry, Jaime,' she whispered.

He leaned back against the pew and cupped the back of her head with his hand, holding her to him. She breathed him in, felt the heat from his body edge the cold fear from hers.

'It's okay, baby. We're okay. We'll find her. There's still a chance.'

She raised her hand to his face, pressed it to his cheek. 'His plan was to kill us all along, Jaime. He came prepared. He never planned to give up Bella at all.' The tears she tried to hold back slipped down her cheeks.

'We don't know that for sure.' His hands cupped her shoulders, and he held her away a little. 'We don't know anything for sure.'

'Where the hell did you get that gun?' Mark drew her to her feet, put an arm around her shoulders and pushed her gently towards the door. 'That's what I'd like to know. Harold, get Jaime to the car. Come on, let's move. You have a lot of explaining to do, Peta. That was a damn stupid move.'

Peta struggled against his grip and dashed the tears away, adrenaline rushing in. 'My only regret is that I missed. I should have killed the bastard.'

'That's enough.' Mark's voice cut through the night. 'You need to tell me where you got that gun. Hand it over now.'

'I have a licence for it.'

'I don't give a rat's arse if you do or don't. Give it to me now. I won't risk you pulling that move again. And I have no desire to see my sister go to jail for murder, whether it's in self-defence or not.'

She pulled it out of her pocket and slapped it into his outstretched palm.

'Thank you. Now we'll have to wait for Paul to make contact again. Let's get back to the hotel and wait there. No doubt it won't be long before we hear from him,' he said. 'Get in the car.'

'I just want my daughter back,' Peta cried.

'Get in the car, Peta.'

She did, letting her brother close the door before taking his own seat in front as Harold started the engine. Jaime slid onto the seat next to her and leaned his head back against the cool vinyl.

'We were so close.' Peta scrubbed angrily at the tears on her cheeks.

Mark shook his head as they drove out of the churchyard. 'I don't believe he would really hurt her. Not even after what happened back there. Even with the evidence, I don't believe he has what he really wants. He needs cash to get him out of the shit with his bikie mates. That will be his next demand.'

'I just want him in jail where he belongs so Bella and I can start again.' Peta clutched the seatbelt where it crossed her chest, squeezing the webbing in her fist.

'It's what we all want.' Jaime reached for her hand.

They made the short drive back to the hotel in silence but Peta's mind churned. It should have been easy. Give Paul what he wanted, get Bella back and move on. But now Jaime was back, and she wasn't sure she could watch him walk away again. When she'd seen him down on the ground and bleeding … all this was her fault. Jaime, Paul, Bella — they were in this mess because of her.

Harold pulled up outside the hotel and Mark escorted them upstairs to the room.

'We'll be back after we've debriefed down at the station. Behave, kids. Jaime, any sign of trouble and you call me, okay? Keep him awake, Peta. He might need an ice pack for that bump.'

Jaime nodded, winced and held a hand to the back of his head. 'I'd settle for a coffee and painkillers.'

'Sit down. I'll make you one.' Peta locked the door behind Mark and then walked over to the kitchen.

Jaime sat down at the benchtop counter and accepted the glass of water she held out to him. She pressed two white tablets from a blister pack and handed them to him before filling the kettle with water and turning it on. Going through the motions, finding the calm. Another game she'd become so good at since meeting Paul. Would she ever have had to do that around Jaime? Was Bella having to employ those same game tactics right now? It wasn't a life skill she'd ever wanted to have to teach her child.

She poured the boiling water onto the granules in the cup and watched them foam. And Jaime. Even amidst the turmoil, it had only taken one look to know that she'd always loved him and always would. Nothing in the world could ever change that.

She stirred in the milk and sugar, her hands unsteady. But their past was messy and their future even more so. She turned and handed him the steaming mug of coffee. Silently, she wrapped her hands around the warmth of her mug and waited. So many questions, so many lies. Would they even be able to tell the difference?

Jaime sighed as he flattened his hands on the counter top. 'You scared the hell out of me, Peta. What were you thinking? If you'd killed him, we'd never know where to look for Bella.'

'It wasn't my intention to kill him. I just wanted to slow him down. Find out where he's hiding my baby. Then I'd kill the bastard.'

'I think you'd have to get in line behind Mark and me for that. Harold might want in on the action too.' He reached out to touch her hand, his fingers trailing across her skin. 'I'm sorry we didn't get Bella back tonight, but I couldn't have lived with myself if something had happened to you out there.'

They sipped their coffee in silence until Peta broke it. 'I found out I was pregnant six weeks after you left. It was a difficult pregnancy and at first they held little hope of survival for the baby.'

'Why didn't you tell me?'

Peta sighed. 'Because I knew you would come back out of a sense of duty,' she replied. 'At the time it didn't seem fair to you. You'd made your decision. The last thing I wanted was to tie you down against your will. Once things settled down, I got on with my life, focused all the love I had left on raising my baby, the little miracle that survived so much before she was even born.'

Peta looked down as his hand covered hers. The long brown fingers were strong and warm. She'd missed the feel of them entwined with hers.

'Does Bella know who her father is?' Jaime asked her.

Peta shook her head and withdrew her hand from his. 'She knows Paul isn't her real father. Please understand, Jaime. I did what I had to do.'

She watched as the expressions flitted across his face and identified with every one of them. Anger, frustration and guilt.

'Neither of us was ready for commitment. I can understand why you didn't want me to know about her. I'm just sorry I've missed so much of her life … of our life.' He paused as he pushed a lock of her hair behind her ear. 'So where do we go from here?'

Peta shrugged. She wished she knew. Until Bella was home safely, she couldn't dream of happy ever afters or even think about the possibility of getting together again. What if all the old obstacles resurfaced and Bella became the pawn in yet another cruel game of adult tug of war when things didn't work out?

'I don't know, Jaime. You're under no obligation. You don't owe me anything and I won't hold you responsible at all. All I ask is that if you don't plan to stay in touch; don't get too involved with her. She's a very vulnerable child and I wouldn't like to see her hurt again,' she said, the warning in her tone unmistakable. 'Paul's done enough damage in our lives as it is. God knows what state she'll be in when we find her.'

Jaime nodded. 'I wish I could change the way things worked out, but I can't.' He retreated to his thoughts, his gaze fixed on the wall across the bench top.

Seeing him again had raised all those buried needs and desires, the hope that he would want to stay and make a life with them as a family. But it had been a long time, and even though she'd never stopped loving him, they were different people now from who they'd been then. There was no reason for him to stay. He'd deserted her, run from the overwhelming responsibility of a relationship built on already shaky ground. Now that responsibility was even greater.

What did he know about raising an almost ten-year-old girl? What did he know about being a father when he couldn't even be a husband first? Peta stole a glance at Jaime's features set in a grim line. No doubt those same questions were flooding his mind.

She clenched the handle of her coffee mug tightly, knuckles white. After a few moments more of silence, he gently prised her fingers loose and laced his between them. She glanced up at him, smiling fleetingly. He pressed a kiss to her knuckles then dropped her hand, standing to take the mugs away and rinse them in the sink. Then he held out a hand and led her to the sofa. Needing to draw on his strength, she abandoned her anger for him, burrowing into his side with her feet curled under her, and let her head sink to his shoulder.

'We'll work it out. Everything will be all right,' he said, kissing her forehead.

Oh God, she hoped that was true. She didn't want to be this close to him. It would be too easy to trust in Jaime and just as easy to be let down again. But his warmth seeped into her cold bones, and she let herself slip into the comfort of it. Her heart wouldn't survive him leaving a second time.

The warmth of his hard body and the smell of his cologne enveloped her as she relaxed against him. His arm came around her, drawing her closer until her forehead rested in the curve of his neck. She inhaled the essence of the man she'd loved for a lifetime. Just for a while, she thought as she snuggled closer, her hand resting on his chest. She'd forgotten how comfortable he was to be around. Her eyes drooped as Jaime's arm tightened and his chin rested against her head.

Chapter Eleven

A yellow moon shone above them, casting an eerie glow on the sand. Waves lapped at their ankles like icy talons clawing and then retreating. Jaime held Peta close.

'Kiss me,' she whispered.

He lowered his head to hers and drank from her lips, hunger deepening his kiss, igniting the desire deep within her. She strained closer, pressed her body into his, needing to feel the full, hard length of him against her.

His lips left hers and sparked a trail down her creamy shoulders. She threw her head back, offering him her neck. Then the dark brown head evolved into a black one and Paul's contorted face stared down at her, his teeth bared in a snarl. Peta screamed and pulled away. She tried to run, but the clawing talons of the sea pulled her back. Her scream turned into a shrill, piercing sound. In the distance, a voice called to her.

'Peta!'

Her eyes snapped open, her heart beating fast. Mark shook her shoulder gently. Desperately she tried to focus. She looked for Jaime, her cheeks warm as she remembered what they'd been doing in her dream, but he wasn't on the sofa with her anymore and instead it was the pillow she hugged.

He sat at the bench top counter and the pounding of her heart settled in time for the shrill ring of her phone to penetrate her confusion. Peta pushed up and grabbed it from the coffee table, panic setting in.

'What?' She dragged a hand through her tangled hair.

Paul's cruel laugh taunted her from the other end of the line. 'Still haven't learned any manners. That wasn't a very wise stunt you pulled last night. I can't believe you shot at me. Lucky for me, you missed. No bloody good at anything as always. Lucky for you, I'm feeling generous. So, I'll give you one last chance. The snivelling little brat is starting to annoy me anyway. All this shit about missing her mummy. Now listen carefully because if you screw it up again, Bella will die.'

'I'm listening.' No more games, no more sticking to the rules. This was one time she couldn't afford to play. 'I'll do what you want. No more games, Paul. I want my daughter back.'

'I want two million dollars. Two hundred thousand in cash and the balance deposited into my bank account by midnight. Deliver the cash to the old homestead on Point Street at ten o'clock tonight.'

'What about Bella?' Peta closed her eyes, her throat tight, fear coiling in her stomach.

'Once I have the money, I will contact you as to her whereabouts. But I'm warning you again … no replay of last night's little fiasco or she dies.'

Her heart contracted, the pain stealing her breath. 'How do I know I can trust you? I want a fair exchange, Paul. That was the agreement.' Not that there'd ever been anything fair in dealings with Paul. There was always only one way. His way.

'Ah, but you broke that agreement, my little dove. When you tried to shoot me.' Peta heard a click on the other end of the line, a sound she associated with the safety latch on a gun, and fear morphed into terror that curled tight hands around her throat.

'No Bella, no deal,' Peta insisted.

'No deal, no Bella.'

'Paul, please give me Bella and I will give you your money, no strings attached.' Peta tried not to sound desperate. 'It will take me a while to organise it with the bank.'

'This is not a trade-off, damn it,' Paul yelled. 'It's my scheme, Peta. We'll do it my way.'

'Let her go now. You'll get what you want, I give you my word.'

'Your word means nothing. You're a lying bitch. You always have been. I told you to get rid of the cops, you didn't. You played games with me again. Now you need to learn your lesson. I mean business, Peta. My life is in danger because of you and now you'll have two lives on your conscience.'

'Danger of your own making, Paul,' Peta snapped. 'You started this by getting involved with those arseholes who own the Tag Raiders, you rat. You sold me out to them —me, my career, the club.'

'You have no idea what Beyond Hell's Reach are capable of. They're bastards, you dumb bitch. When they're done stripping my flesh, they'll come looking for you. What I've done is a piece of piss compared to what they've got planned for you. None of this would have been necessary if you'd just been a good little wife and handed over the money you owed me,' Paul snapped.

'I owed you?' Incredulous, she placed a hand on her head, willing the throb of a headache to stop. 'I made that money through hard work. I gave you money to set up the business. I paid you to be my manager. How do I owe you?'

'You owe me for the nights that you denied me entry to your bed. For the years you spent pining for your boyfriend on my time. For me giving you the chance to be a star,' Paul spat at her.

'You gave up your rights when you beat me.' Peta felt her patience slipping.

'I'm done talking. You listen or your daughter dies. Bring the money to the homestead on Point Street and I'll give you Bella back.' The line went dead in her ear.

Peta listened to the silence hanging heavy in the air. What if she couldn't arrange the money in time? She was in Williams for God's sake. This was the sort of thing she needed to be in the city for, her own branch, her own bank manager. You couldn't transfer a sum of money like that by direct transfer.

'Do you have the money?' Mark asked, frowning.

Peta nodded, twisting her hands. 'It can be arranged. I'll need to contact my bank manager.'

'We need a plan to make sure the bastard doesn't get away again.' Harold joined the conversation.

'And make sure we get Bella back this time and that he doesn't just take off with the money,' Mark agreed.

Peta looked at her watch, panic a pool of acid in her stomach. They must have slept for longer than she'd thought. It was mid-morning. 'We need to get to a bank.'

'Paul must be in a lot of trouble to need that kind of money. The people he's involved with don't play games. They'll get him one way or another. He's put them in danger with this little scheme of his and they won't take a chance on it happening again,' said Mark. 'All they want is their money back and the evidence destroyed. They won't care who gets hurt in the process. He'll be safer in jail. Out of jail, he's a dead man. It's only a matter of time. My guess is Beyond Hell's Reach are behind this whole kidnapping thing. They know the law and what you have will see their whole operation end in turmoil. They want the evidence destroyed and Paul is the decoy. Not even their lawyers could make this one go away.'

Peta shivered. 'Once they have the evidence, he's as good as dead. Maybe I should just shoot him myself and save them the trouble.'

'Yes, we still need to talk about that little stunt you pulled last night. I had a hard time explaining that one to the chief. Bella will be fine, Peta. Paul must have her with him most of the time, or at least somewhere nearby. He can't take the risk of whoever is after him getting hold of her. I honestly don't think he would put her life in danger,' Mark reassured her. 'We'll find her.'

'So, you're thinking we set him up when Peta drops off the cash?' Jaime moved to put his arm around Peta's shoulders.

She leaned into him, needing the warmth and comfort. How had it come to this?

'Chances are he has her at the homestead where he wants you to drop off the cash. I know the place. It's old and no-one lives in it anymore. Part of an estate waiting to be settled because the owner died with no will and no family. It's comfortable, furnished and has access to running water, even though the electricity was cut when the owner passed away. Being that far out of town though, there'd be a generator around somewhere to give the place power,' Harold said. 'He's running out of time and places to hide. I say we move in now.'

'What if Bella's not there?' asked Jaime.

Oh God, she had to be. Please let her be there. Peta fisted a hand in his shirt. He covered it with his own.

'She will be. He'll be watching for that cash and planning a quick getaway,' said Mark. 'He won't want to hang around. My guess is he already has a ticket to somewhere he won't be found.'

Harold snorted. 'As if they won't find him wherever he goes.'

'That's why we have to find him first.' Mark reached for his keys. 'You two stay here. Don't leave the room. Harold, we need to round up the boys and get some back up in from Collie.'

Unease trickled up Peta's spine. Nothing they'd done so far had run to plan. 'What about the money?'

Mark pressed a kiss to her cheek. 'We won't need the money. We're not waiting any longer. Not when he's told us where she is.'

Panic pushed the unease away. 'No! You heard what he said. He'll kill her. We have to do it his way. We can't risk Bella being caught up in the middle of an ambush.'

'Hostage negotiation.'

'Semantics. Mark, you know hostage negotiation seldom ends well. Someone always gets hurt.'

'Not on my watch.' He turned to leave. 'Stay out of trouble until we get back. We'll be a couple of hours getting things organised. You'll need to be there when we go in just in case he demands to talk to you. We'll be back for you as soon as we have a plan of attack mapped out.'

'I don't like it,' Peta said as the door closed behind them.

Jaime walked her over to the sofa. 'Your brother knows what he's doing. He's the best there is.'

'That doesn't make this right.' She sat, her nerves balled in a knot in her stomach. 'I'm scared, Jaime.'

The cushions dipped under his weight as he sat next to her and gathered her onto his lap. 'Then we'll hold each other until it's over. Tell me about Bella.'

Her nerves were wired and the last thing she felt like was chit chat, but if it made the time go faster until she got her daughter back, she would. She settled against him as he sat back, listened to the comfort of his heartbeat and told him about the little girl who'd seen more than a ten-year-old should.

~

Jaime listened as Peta told him about his daughter, from her favourite colour to her oldest, most treasured toy — the bear he'd won at the annual fair for Peta too many years ago to count. Love for the little girl grew in his heart. He hoped Mark's plan worked because God knows, he wanted to meet his daughter. There was no one he trusted more to bring her home safely.

Then she spoke about the horror of her marriage to Paul, the ups and downs of her career, and the fear she'd lived through when crooked lawyers, Bennetti and Albero, and Beyond Hell's Reach started visiting the nightclub. He talked her through it while he eased the tension in her shoulders and rubbed her back in soothing circles.

Peta relaxed in his arms, her fingers playing with the buttons on his shirt as she spoke, each stroke against his chest teasing his senses. He shouldn't want to kiss her right now, not until this was over. But hadn't they wasted enough time? He'd held her while she slept, fallen in love with her strength, never fallen out of love with the woman she was.

He tipped up her chin. Her gaze flew to his, realisation and acceptance of his intentions clear in its depth. Meeting with no resistance, he touched his lips to hers, felt her mouth move under his and kissed her with everything in his heart. Her hand came up to touch his cheek and he loved the feel of it there, so he placed his over hers and pressed it closer.

She pulled back a fraction. 'Jaime?'

What did she need? He had no words for the past and no plan for the future, but he'd give her whatever she needed from him right now. He pressed his forehead to hers.

'Maybe it's not the right time,' he whispered.

'Maybe it's the perfect time.'

'It shouldn't be with everything going on.'

'Or maybe we both need comfort.'

Sadness edged his smile. 'I won't have comfort sex with you.'

'Then don't.'

She ran her fingers over his mouth, and he figured he'd take whatever she offered. So, when her lips took his, he gave her kisses. When her hands explored the contours of his chest, he returned the favour. When her fingers found the zipper on his jeans and drew it down, he let her. And when things got too hot on the sofa, he carried her to bed and showed her commitment not comfort.

Chapter Twelve

eta turned away from Jaime's warmth as he slept and slipped to the edge of the mattress. Now he knew everything. She had no more secrets from him. He'd listened to her stories, witnessed the scars, caressed them with his lips and promised her no one would ever hurt her again. Still doubt lingered.

If he changed his mind, wanted Bella but not her, she'd placed the power in his hands. Handed him the reason to take her daughter away. She'd gone to bed with him, seen to her own pleasures, while Bella was in the hands of a maniac. What responsible mother did that? She squeezed her eyes shut against the guilt that battered her heart.

Please God, make this nightmare end. She'd abandoned all hope of ever having a normal life for her and her little girl. Bella deserved so much more than she could give. She deserved a family, brothers and sisters, happiness, a normal childhood. Things she'd never had.

Being in Jaime's arms again … heaven. No amount of shame or guilt could take that away. All it proved was she loved him now more than she had before. That the years apart had done little to change her feelings for him. In his arms, she felt safe. Felt like she had a chance to belong. But until Bella was back in her arms, she couldn't belong anywhere.

The mattress dipped as Jaime reached for her, his fingers playing on her back. 'Where'd you go? Come back here for a while.'

Peta sat up and his hand dropped to the sheets as she moved out of reach. The temptation to roll back into his arms was strong, but she'd be wiser to face reality. Take this memory and treasure it to keep her warm on the cold nights when she was alone again.

'Mark and Harold will be back soon. I'm going to have a shower and get ready.' She stood, pulled his old shirt from the chair near the window and slipped it on, clutching the loose front in her fist.

He pushed himself up on his elbows, his gaze following her as she walked around the end of the bed. 'You okay?'

She stopped at the door to the room. Okay? No, she'd never be that again. Of all the stupid things she'd done in her life, this capped it. She'd been lured by his patience and understanding, succumbed to his touch like the desperate and needy young girl she'd once been, fallen in love all over again with the man who might leave them behind a second time. Peta shivered. 'I'm fine.' And she would be. They would be, her and Bella, she'd make sure of it.

'Talk to me.'

'I need to be ready, Jaime. I can't let Paul win this leg. This is the last chance I have to get Bella back. He'll snap if I don't. I can't let that happen.'

Would he push the issue? Was he going to analyse what had happened between them? Make promises he couldn't keep? Please God, don't let him, because talk was cheap and actions counted, and if he reached for her again, she wouldn't be able to say no. Jaime represented everything she wanted and couldn't have. Getting in deeper would be a huge mistake.

The bed sheets rustled as he moved. She turned, her back to the closed door, her hands spread against the wood behind her. He sat on the edge of the mattress, gloriously naked, arms extended behind him as his beautiful big, comforting hands balanced his weight.

'No, we won't let that happen. Go and do what you have to, Peta.' He leaned forward, hands on his knees. 'But when Bella is safe, we need to talk about us.'

'There is no us.'

Anger flashed in his eyes. 'So, this —' he waved a hand over the rumpled sheets '— this meant nothing at all to you?'

It meant everything and more. It meant hope, dreams and fantasies come true, but nothing she could let herself hold onto. She dropped her gaze from his. He'd always been able to read her too well. 'I didn't say that.'

He stood, walked over to her as she raised her eyes to watch the sway of his hips, the ripple of muscle in his legs and the hands that reached for her waist and urged her closer. 'Then there's hope for us.' His arms slipped around her, and she let her head rest against his shoulder. 'I won't let you handle this alone anymore.'

Peta closed her eyes to the press of his lips against her temple and wrapped her arms around his waist. One last hold before she let him go. *If you love someone, set them free* ... She'd lived by that quote for so long. *If they come back to you, they're yours* ... He was back, but he wasn't hers to keep. Not yet. Maybe never.

She pushed out of his hold and his arms fell away from around her as he stepped back. Her heart flooded with love for him. He'd always instinctively known when to give her space. With one last look at his face, she etched it in her memory for a time when she wouldn't see it anymore and turned to open the door.

With a sigh, Jaime watched the door close behind Peta then he moved back to the bed and hunted out his jocks. He felt like an absolute dick for getting angry with her.

Convincing Peta he was in it for the long haul would take some time. She had no reason to believe it, no evidence of his staying power beyond surviving two attacks by her ex-husband. Survival not staying power, not the proof she needed that he would stand by her and his child. Would have done so years ago, if she'd asked.

The outer door to the suite squeaked on hinges needing oil and signalled the return of Mark and Harold. Jaime tugged on his shirt and jeans. Show time. Today was the day he'd meet his daughter for the first time. If only it were under different circumstances. And if Paul had harmed a hair on her head, he'd better hope Harold and Mark got to him first. If they didn't, he'd be the one waiting for visiting hours in a maximum-security prison.

Pulling open the bedroom door, he brushed a hand through his hair, took a deep breath and hoped Mark had brought coffee.

Eyebrows raised, Mark handed him a large takeaway cup. 'Where's Peta?'

'Shower.' Jaime sipped, wincing as the liquid scorched his lip. 'This isn't your average fast-food shit. Fuck me.'

'You're not my type, but obviously you're someone else's.' Mark's gaze travelled over his shoulder to the rumpled bed visible through the open door.

'Mind your own business.' Jaime lifted the plastic lid on the cup and blew over the hot coffee.

'She is my business. At least until we have my niece back and Price in custody.'

'Great. Well, I hope you have a plan for that. I'd like to see it when you're finished judging.' Jaime secured the lid back in place.

'Protecting.'

'Don't play word games with me. Give me the run down.'

Mark sipped his own coffee, slowly and thoughtfully. Jaime could almost hear the cogs turning. 'A team has gone ahead to carry out surveillance. Any activity and they'll radio in. He's small fry, so we don't need big numbers to take him down. Just a good shot in case things go wrong, which Harold here is the best at.'

'What about his mates from Beyond Hell's Reach?'

'They won't show up. They'll stay out of it. He's high risk. They can't afford to be caught in the crossfire for a couple of million. Their drug business is worth far more than the debt Paul owes them.'

'And they have their own justice system for when he ends up in lock up.' A kangaroo court that usually ended up with the guilty party seriously injured. Or dead. Jaime grimaced. The outcome wouldn't be pleasant for Price either way.

'Exactly. So, we move in about an hour from now. Try negotiation.'

'Will that put Bella at risk?' Every moment counted

in a hostage negotiation, and if Price was already on the edge of desperation, he'd do anything to save his arse.

'I wouldn't be doing this if I thought it would. Price will have a target painted on any body part that will end all threat quickly. My boys will shoot to kill if they have to.' Mark's expression turned grim. 'I'd rather they didn't have to.'

'There's a part of me that wishes they did.'

'Yeah, I get that, but red tape, paperwork — much easier to keep him alive. Harold, where's that map?'

Harold spread a map out on the kitchen bench top, his powerful hands with their thick fingers pointing out the markings. Not a man Jaime or any criminal in their right mind would want to mess with. 'We'll have men positioned in the spots marked with red dots, all armed, all trained shots.'

Peta walked in quietly, her footsteps making little or no sound, but Jaime picked up on the scent of her favourite shampoo and the essence of her that was everything he loved. He tried to ignore her presence as he studied the map, but she slipped in between him and Harold, the gap too small for her body not to brush against his.

He pushed up onto the bar chair and gathered her into the V of his legs, his heart hitching when she didn't resist. He folded his arms around her and drew her back against him. Comfort, that's all she needed. Maybe it was all he needed.

'Where will I be?' Her hand brushed over the map, slightly unsteady.

'As far out of the way as possible.' Mark shot her a warning look. 'You stay in the car. The only time you get out is if I tell you to. The only reason you're there at all is in case he wants to speak to you.'

'And when he releases Bella.'

She shivered against Jaime, and he hugged her hard. 'We'll get her out this time.' He hoped to God he was right.

Chapter Thirteen

eta's heart pounded, her throat tight, her palms damp and the urge to run up to the front door and confront Paul too strong to ignore.

Afternoon heat shimmered off the landscape surrounding the abandoned homestead as Mark killed the engine and coasted to a stop up the long, overgrown drive. A short distance away, an eerie silence had settled around the building itself, the dusty windows dark and empty beneath the wraparound verandah.

'Stay in the car. Harold and I will get a little closer.'

'No. I'm not staying here alone. I'm coming too.' She didn't want to think of the awful things Paul was capable of if he found her alone. Too often she'd felt the brute force of his anger.

'God damn it, Peta, stay.' Mark's frustration was

clear in the way he shoved a hand through his hair. Time was running out. 'Jaime, stay with her.'

Fear gripped Peta; her stomach churned. This was too close. Paul would know they were setting a trap for him. As the car doors closed quietly behind Harold and Mark, she clung to Jaime's hand, unease eating away at her stomach. He squeezed her fingers reassuringly.

In silence, they watched Mark and Harold move closer under the cover of overgrowth, guns securely in their hands. Giant ghost gums cast shadows in the receding sunlight, the natural wild beauty of the property marred by the violence Paul had brought to it. Peta shivered. A kangaroo dashed across the field behind the homestead, scaring a flock of pink cockatoos into flight. She moved closer to Jaime.

His arm came around her shoulders. 'We're fine. It's just a roo.'

But the knot coiling in her chest warned her it was more. She'd felt this fear before. Hiding. In a cupboard, under the bed, anywhere where Paul couldn't find her. Waiting until he'd given up looking.

She looked for Mark and Harold, but they'd gone, blending into the landscape as they edged closer to the homestead. Under her hand, Jaime's thigh tensed. He felt it too. The same evil presence, the same sensation of being watched. He cast a quick look around him, through the front windscreen, out the rear, to either side.

Jaime pulled his arm from around her. 'Stay in the car. I'm going to get out and have a look, okay?'

'No!' She tightened her grip on his leg. 'You have no protection. Nothing to defend yourself with if he comes for you.'

'I have my hands, honey. I know how to use them.'

'Oh God, I want this to end.'

He leaned over and kissed her forehead. 'It will be over soon.'

As he reached for the handle, the door was ripped from his grip and the sound of a rifle being cocked echoed through Peta's ears.

'Get out.'

Jaime squeezed Peta's hand before he obeyed Paul's command. She followed him out the door, bile bitter in her throat. Paul kept the rifle trained on them as they moved.

'Walk. Dead ahead.'

He shoved them in a direction up the hill away from the homestead. Peta's heart pounded. He'd kill them this time, no doubt about it. The glassed look, the enlarged pupils that made his brown eyes a sea of black. She'd seen it before. He was high. With it came brute strength, no ability to reason and murderous paranoia. What price was freedom from this nightmare?

Paul pointed to the solid steel structure of an old sea container. 'Open the doors.'

Jaime obeyed and lifted the lever, but she felt the

control in his body as he moved, saw the blank mask on his face. It did nothing to settle her fear knowing that behind that mask he'd be scanning, assessing, logging details. Playing the game. He knew it too.

Paul kept the rifle squarely aimed between Jaime's shoulder blades with one hand and shoved Peta onto the floor with the other.

'Mummy,' Bella cried out and made a move to go to her.

'Stay where you are, Bella,' Paul barked. 'Well, look what we have here. A nice little family reunion.'

Peta rubbed her knee. Her elbow burned from the impact with the hard floor. 'What more do you want, Paul? You have what you wanted. You have all the evidence against you.'

'I told you I wanted money. I gave you clear instructions. You didn't listen.'

'Keeping us prisoner will ensure you go to jail. Mark is out there. He'll find us, find you.' Playing the game no longer counted. Not when Paul was too out of his mind to play too.

'Who said anything about keeping you prisoner? That means keeping you alive. So brave, dishing out fighting words. I guess I'll have to beat you into submission again.' He raised his hand to carry out his threat.

'Give it your best shot. You're a coward. A slimy

little coward who has to beat up women and children because he can't get his kicks any other way.'

'Peta!' Jaime's warning cut through the air as Paul's face coloured with rage. 'That's enough.'

Her heart pounded at the thought of the damage Paul would do this time. She wouldn't survive it, but it would give Jaime the opportunity to fight without a rifle at his back.

'Well, that's the most sensible thing you've said all day, Caruso. Now I'll leave you all to get re-acquainted, shall I? Don't get too comfortable though. Your reunion will be short-lived.' Paul prodded Jaime inside, keeping his aim steady as he backed out of the container. 'First I have a score to settle with Perth's finest.'

They listened to the metallic echo as the lever descended to lock the doors and the rattle of a chain clang against the metal. In the dim light of a bare overhead light, Bella rushed over, throwing her arms around Peta's waist and sobbing into her shirtfront. Peta held her tightly.

'Are you okay, baby? Did he hurt you?' she asked, her voice shaking.

Bella shook her head. 'I'm okay, Mummy. I'm just scared when Paul's so mean.'

'Good girl. Brave girl.' With a hug for Bella, Peta looked at Jaime. 'What do we do now?'

'What were you thinking taunting him like that, Peta? He could have knocked you unconscious without a second thought. And make no mistake, he would have.' Jaime's mask slipped as anger burned in its place.

'He didn't and I'm okay. Focus on that. We have to find a way out of here. Paul is close to snapping. He's high. When he is, he's uncontrollable and dangerous.' Where were Mark and Harold? If Paul snuck up the way he had on her and Jaime, the others were in danger too. 'I can't risk Bella's safety any longer.' She paused to sit against the wall and hug Bella more closely. 'I knew he'd be waiting. I've lived with him long enough to know how his mind works. He won't stop until he has what he wants.'

Jaime pressed his fingers to his eyes. 'If he doesn't get what he wants, he'll kill us all so there's nobody left to testify against him.' He moved to sit next to her on the floor.

'Paul doesn't have the balls to do it himself. He'll have his buddies, Beyond Hell's Reach, do it for him. They've done it before.' The chill in her voice dropped the temperature in the container several degrees. 'Or he'll leave us here to die. Mark and Harold have their focus on the homestead. They won't be looking for a sea container. That's if he doesn't finish them off first.'

'I hope they're smarter than that.' Jaime muttered an oath under his breath. Looking at Bella huddled in Peta's arms, her face buried against her shirt. 'And until they come looking for us, we're at the mercy of a drug-addicted psychopath. This whole situation is out of hand. How did it get this far?'

'I let it. I should have done something about its years ago and I didn't.' Peta reached out and touched him. 'I hate how you got involved in all this and I'm sorry. This isn't your fight.'

Jaime stared at her. 'It's a bit late to walk away now. There's too much at stake here.'

'I told you, you don't owe me anything.' Anger coloured her cheeks.

'No,' he answered coldly, 'but I'm not thinking in terms of debt. Let's leave this discussion for later. Right now, we need to find a way out of here.' Jaime looked around.

'When Mark and Harold realise what's happened and come after Paul, they'll walk right into another trap.' Peta's whisper echoed in the silence. 'If they make it at all.' She hated the thread of defeat in her words.

'Don't give up now, sweetheart. Your brother is smart. He'll be all over this with a plan.' Jaime reached for her hand and gave it a squeeze. 'Come closer,' he said, tugging gently.

Peta didn't hesitate as she shifted herself and Bella closer. Jaime placed a comforting arm around them. How would they get out of this? This problem with Paul had gone on long enough. He'd endangered her life, her daughter's life and the lives of the people who mattered most to her. The more she thought about it, the fiercer the anger became, quickly overriding the fear that had consumed her earlier. She'd had enough of living in fear of a man who was really much weaker in character than herself, a bully who worked with his fists and emotional blackmail to get what he wanted from life.

In his present state of mind though, he was unstable and dangerous, and possibly a little scared himself. The harder she thought, the more she realised the extent of Paul's own danger. Even if he eliminated all of them, his own chances of survival were slim. Bennetti, Albero and Beyond Hell's Reach were unforgiving of failure. And that put the lives of the kids in the Tag Raiders gang at risk too. If the evidence got out, they wouldn't hesitate to make the four teenage runners' deaths look like accidents to cover up their trail of drugs, money laundering and destruction.

The chain rattled against the door of the container and the lever slammed up. Paul threw the doors open, his expression murderous as he rushed in, the rifle replaced by a handgun. All thought for survival and escape fled, replaced by the cold, merciless grip of fear on her spine. Fading sunlight filled the dark reaches of the container. Peta pulled away from Jaime, her arms instinctively tightening around Bella as she whimpered.

'You bitch!' The cold, hard steel of a gun pressed up hard under her chin. The tip of the barrel dug mercilessly into the soft tissue below her jaw.

Terror tore through her as Peta pushed a shaking Bella off her lap. 'Go, baby.'

She crawled away but Peta couldn't see to where. *Please God, don't let him hurt her.*

'They've got the fucking place surrounded.' Paul's hands were in her hair, dragging her head back, smacking it against the steel wall.

Out the corner of her eye she saw Jaime shift. The movement caught Paul's attention and he swung the gun across.

'Don't you fucking move, Caruso!'

A deafening sound echoed off the metal walls around them, ringing in her ears, as the gun discharged. Peta saw Jaime jerk and pull up his knee.

Anger built in Peta's stomach like a red-hot burning coal, raging through her with fierce intensity. 'You bastard! What the hell is wrong with you? You've just shot a man. You could have shot Bella. You could have killed my daughter.'

Peta felt Paul's grip on her hair slack off, the hand that held the gun shook. Adrenaline chased the anger through her bloodstream as she grabbed Paul's arm where the gun trembled in his hand. She struggled against his weight advantage, managed to keep the gun from pointing in Bella's direction.

Jaime surged to his feet, forcing Paul's arm back, and brought the heel of his boot down heavily on Paul's instep.

Paul swore furiously as bones crunched in his foot. Jaime brought his knee up under Paul's wrist, bringing his arm down with a crack that turned Peta's stomach, forcing him to drop the gun.

Paul gripped his wrist against his chest. 'Son of a bitch! You broke my arm.'

Horror etched into his face. She knew he wouldn't be feeling the pain yet. Not until the effects of whatever he'd snorted had worn off.

Peta kicked the gun away as Jaime forced Paul into a headlock, the red stain of blood on his pants growing around his thigh and sweat glistening on his face. Fear coursed through her as she looked around for Bella. Her little girl huddled in the corner, tight as a ball, as small as she could make herself. 'Good girl. Stay there.'

Disabled by Jaime's arm cutting off his air supply, Paul struggled. Peta moved quickly, picking up the gun and aiming it at the top of Paul's head as Jaime maintained his hold.

'Mark,' she yelled, hoping her brother was in earshot. That they'd heard the gun go off. 'Don't move, Paul, or I swear to God I'll shoot you.'

Paul straightened and tried to take a swing at Jaime with his good arm. He blocked the blow, twisting Paul's arm back and then upwards. Jaime's boot to the backs of his knees brought him down heavily, face first. Grasping both hands behind Paul's back, he forced them up, immobilizing him, his scream of pain and the crunching bones in his broken arm echoing in the confined space. Then Jaime rammed his knee down heavily on Paul's lower spine, not giving him chance to draw strength or a breath between moves as he anchored him down with his body weight. Paul writhed under him, a man broken by his own misdeeds.

'Now you know how it feels, you coward,' she muttered, holding the gun trained on him. 'Not so great to be on the receiving end, is it?' She looked at Jaime. 'You okay?'

'I will be when your brother gets his arse up here.' He ground his teeth and winced as Paul had one last attempt at dislodging him. Looking around, he spotted a plastic jar filled with cable ties in the corner Bella was huddled in. 'Bring me that jar, Bell. That's a good girl.'

She unfurled herself from the corner and pushed the jar across. It toppled, spilling the cable ties on the floor near him. He reached for them and quickly tied Paul's hands together and then his feet. 'Trussed up like the pig you are.' He patted the man's head and pushed to his feet. 'All we're missing is the apple in your mouth. Sweet Jesus, Peta. That was a damn risky move. Remind me never to pick an argument with you,' he muttered. 'You can put the gun down now. He's not going anywhere.'

She lowered the gun, and he took it from her, removing the cartridge and putting it in his pocket. 'He shot you.' Her hands shook.

'Yes, left thigh. Right between the legs. A few inches higher and it could have been a different outcome,' he muttered as he dropped to his knees. 'Adrenaline's wearing off. It's gonna hurt like buggery.'

'Lie down.' Peta knelt next to Jaime and inspected his wound. So much blood. She had to stop the bleeding. If she lost him now … Hopefully Paul was a lousy shot. Surely if he'd hit anything major, Jaime wouldn't still be talking? Running back over to Paul, she tore a strip off the back of his shirt big enough to act as a bandage.

'Hey,' Paul shouted, 'Do you have any idea how much that shirt cost me?'

'Shut up or I'll use the rest of it to stuff in your mouth.' She knelt back over Jaime's leg and wrapped the material around the wound, securing it with a knot and checking it wasn't too tight. Where the bloody hell was Mark? 'Stay with me, Jaime. For God's sake, don't even think about closing your eyes.' She stood and turned to Bella. 'Come here, baby.' She held her arms open and hugged her daughter tightly. 'I'm so sorry you had to see that.' She kissed Bella's head. Relief flooded her heart. Bella was safe. She had her baby back.

'I was so scared, Mummy.'

'I hate that you were scared, baby.'

'Not anymore.' She looked at Jaime properly for the first time since they'd been thrown into the shipping container. 'Mummy, who is he?' she whispered.

Peta's heart skipped a beat. Should she tell her daughter the truth? Oh, good lord, if she did, her baby might get her hopes up. Relief washed over her as she heard the pounding of footsteps rushing towards them, Mark's voice shouting orders. Their battles were far from over, but the worst had passed.

Mark and Harold appeared cautiously in the doorway, guns drawn as they took in the scene. 'Looks like the excitement's over.'

'Took you long enough. Need an ambulance. Maybe two. Feeling a little woozy here.' Jaime stretched out on the floor, leg bent at the knee to take the pressure off his heart, his eyes glued to Peta and Bella as if they would be the last sight he'd ever see.

'I'll take care of it.' Harold backed out the door.

'Are you okay?' Mark came over. 'Ouch. Not good. A few inches higher and …'

'Stuff it.' Jaime groaned.

'Who did that?' Mark nodded to where Paul lay squirming and moaning on the floor.

Bella pointed to Jaime. 'He did, Uncle Mark. Even when he was hurt. I think he's a superhero.'

Mark raised his eyebrows at Jaime who grimaced. 'All in a day's work. Get us out of here now.'

Mark nodded. 'Well done. Might have to ask you some questions about it though. I don't suppose you want a job on the force?'

Jaime rolled his head from side to side on the floor. 'No. Don't need any more excitement. I want to take my family home.'

Chapter Fourteen

Not even pretending to be gentle, Harold hauled Paul up off the floor onto his knees by the collar of his shirt and undid the cable ties around his ankles. 'If you so much as twitch your big toe, you're in shit. Ambulance is on the way.' He pushed Paul ahead of him out the container, stopping for a moment in front of Peta. 'Last chance to apologise for being a dick.'

'That's the last time you'll ever abuse me again, Paul.'

Paul spat on the floor at Peta's feet. 'When I get out, I'm coming to get you,' he promised. 'You'll never be safe, you stupid bitch.'

Peta arched an eyebrow at him. 'If you survive dropping the soap in the shower block, I'll be waiting so

I can kick your sorry arse until you learn your miserable lesson. Unlike Jaime, I'll shoot first and ask questions later. The girl you used to push around is gone for good.'

Mark cleared his throat and gently steered Peta away. 'Threatening your attacker is probably not wise,' he said. 'Lucky his arms aren't much use and that was off the record.'

Peta looked up at him. Relief rushed through her. It was over. Bella was safe. They were alive. 'Yes, I know, but payback is such a great reward.'

'Can't argue with that.' Mark nodded. 'Will you guys ride with Jaime?'

Peta nodded. She wanted Bella checked over by the paramedics anyway and to make sure Jaime survived the trip okay. She had so much to say, so much to thank him for, but it would have to wait.

Jaime reached for Peta's hand. She clasped it and squeezed tightly. When Paul had the gun trained on Jaime she'd realised that no matter how much she tried to ignore it, she loved him. Not the adolescent love she'd once had for him, but a more overpowering, all-consuming kind. The kind of love she knew he couldn't give in return because he still needed his freedom. If he left them now their lives would never be the same again.

Peta sighed. There would never be anyone else for her but Jaime. There never had been. But she was damned if she'd allow him to stay out of a sense of duty. Peta's heart burned as tears threatened at the back of her throat. He needed to know it was okay to leave, that she didn't plan on making any demands on him.

'The ambulance is here. Peta, they'll give you and Bella a quick check up, okay?'

'I'm fine. Bella needs checking.'

'Humour me.' Mark kissed the top of her head and handed her over as the paramedics entered the container.

She suffered through the check up for Bella, who held her hand while another paramedic took care of her. Jaime now lay unmoving on the stretcher inside the ambulance. Peta watched as they inserted a needle into his arm and attached a drip. Please God, let him be okay.

The ambulance drew to a halt at the emergency room and all thoughts swept away as the doors opened to release the response staff. The porter wheeled Jaime away, flocked by a nurse with a clipboard, rattling off questions. He disappeared through the doors as Peta and Bella were ushered into a waiting room.

Bella's head drifted to Peta's shoulder as thoughts began to churn in her head again. There'd be a court case, a conviction, and God knew what else as Mark unravelled the ties of Paul's connection to Bennetti and

Albero, but her nightmare was almost over and then she and Bella could start afresh. With or without Jaime.

'Mrs Caruso?' The surgeon stepped into the waiting room.

She didn't attempt to correct him. It didn't matter. All that mattered was that Jaime would be okay. 'Yes?'

'Surgery went well. The bullet entered above the knee on the right front of the thigh and exited out the left. He's a lucky man. It missed the femur and femoral artery, so just some muscle and nerve damage. He'll make a full recovery with some rehabilitation.'

Relief surged through her. 'Thank you.' Finally, some good news.

'He's awake. You may see him now. The nurse will take you through.'

'Thank you.'

Peta woke Bella and they followed the nurse to the ward where Jaime lay. Her heart did a little dance of relief at the grin on his pale face.

'Hey, you guys okay?'

Even croaky from the anaesthetic, the sound of his voice could weaken her knees, the concern in his dark eyes warming her heart. Relief that he was okay warred with the regret of having to watch him walk away again when all this was over.

Bella eyed him shyly before going to his side and planting a kiss on his cheek. 'We're okay. You were really brave. You're my hero.'

Jaime smiled. 'I think your mum's the hero in this one, Bella. She never gave up looking for you.'

Bella nodded. 'She's the coolest mum in the world. You should marry her.'

Warmth crept into Peta's cheeks. 'Bella, you can't say things like that, darling. How are you feeling, Jaime?'

'Do I take that as a no?' Jaime's grin faded. 'I'm just a little sore in every possible spot on my body. How about you guys?'

'We're fine. We'll let you rest now.'

A shadow passed over Jaime's face. 'Peta, we need to talk. We need to sort this thing out. Now that this business with Paul is settled —' He broke off as Mark stepped into the room.

Mark's expression was dark as he drew nearer the bedside. He placed an arm around Peta's shoulder and hugged her quickly before releasing her again. 'I'm afraid it's not over yet,' he informed them. 'It seems Paul didn't finish the job they assigned him to do. Couldn't quite make the kill. Beyond Hell's Reach are looking for you, and it's not for a friendly chat. We need to get you out of the way fast.'

Peta's heart launched into her throat. No, the nightmare wasn't over yet. 'When will it end?'

'Why should it when they can get away with destroying people's lives dealing in the crap they put out on the streets? Those kids in the Tag Raiders gang will grow up to be dealers or die homeless on the street from an overdose. That's the reality of this. You know what's on that video — the people involved and the far reach of their crimes — you'll be a target until you're lying on a cold slab in the morgue unless I can take these guys down at their core.'

'I know the consequences.' Tears strangled the words that should have been a shout.

Jaime reached out to thread his fingers through hers. 'They'll come after us because we know too much.'

'Exactly. Paul had no idea what he was getting into when he got involved with these thugs. We have to do this the right way, Peta. Take them out completely or they'll do this to someone else. I'm sure you don't want that to happen.' Mark held her chin and forced her to look at him. 'We've got this far, let's not waste it.'

Peta swiped at the tears of frustration with her free hand. In her heart she knew they were right. 'What do we have to do?'

'Good girl.' Mark squeezed her shoulder. 'I've organised transport out of here to one of the safety houses we use for the witness protection program. Unfortunately, we can't risk sending a nurse along for Jaime, so you'll have to take care of him. The instructions and medical supplies are already loaded and ready to go.'

He pulled a wheelchair closer to the bed. Jaime gave Peta's fingers a squeeze before releasing her hand. He lifted himself off the pillows and let Mark help him off the bed into the wheelchair.

'Hurry, guys. Word is they're on their way to town already. If you're gone, they'll leave quietly. Peta, you take Jaime, I'll take Bella.' He picked up a pair of crutches from next to the bed and handed them to Jaime. 'Hold onto these. You'll need them when we leave the wheelchair behind.'

Peta pushed Jaime's chair out into the corridor while Mark followed behind her carrying Bella. She sensed the tension in him, noted his hyper awareness of their surroundings. This couldn't be happening. Dread settled in her stomach like cold, heavy porridge. She'd seen the atrocities Paul's associates were capable of, knew the consequences and outcomes, had heard the rumours of their ties to outlawed gangs, and experienced firsthand the violence they promoted as justice.

They waited for the elevator, and fear became a bitter taste in Peta's throat once again. When the doors finally opened, Mark punched the button on the control panel for the top floor. He hurried them out of the elevator onto the roof where Harold waited with the emergency rescue chopper.

'Not sure this is a wise move, mate, putting them in isolation together. Bet you a beer it doesn't help them sort things out.'

Peta settled Jaime and Bella inside the helicopter and tried to ignore the conversation between the two men. Mark's intentions had always been good, but he needed to let this go. Things would never be the same between her and Jaime again. Ever.

Harold fiddled with his collar, loosening the top buttons. 'I don't want to be doing a murder investigation on witnesses in protection.'

'It's more important that they're safe together. Anything else that comes from this is a bonus. Besides, Jaime can take care of himself. I'm sure he has ways of diffusing my sister's temper.' Mark grinned.

Harold grimaced. 'You should stick to detective work. As fairy godmother matchmakers go, you're pretty damn rough around the edges.'

Mark laughed. 'Take this baby away, Harold. You've got witnesses to get to safety. Go fly a chopper.'

'I like a good light brew, by the way. I've got this bet in the bag.'

'The way I see it, the drinks are on you. Call it a cop's hunch,' Mark called after Harold as he headed for the helicopter.

She'd love to tell him what to do with his bet and his beers, but she couldn't. Not when she knew he was only doing what he thought was best for everyone. She'd had to trust his instincts in the past, and she had no reason not to do the same now, no matter what his hidden agenda was. Life would make the choice for them. The tilt of Jaime's lips said he'd heard too. She refused to return his smile.

The loud sweep of blades followed the engine firing to life and before long Williams faded into the distance as the chopper cut through the sky. Peta breathed a sigh of relief. An hour later they landed at an airstrip she recognised as a local Perth airfield for small business flights and were quickly transferred to a Beechcraft Baron. Harold took the controls, which left Peta and Jaime alone. Exhausted, Bella cuddled up under a blanket next to her father's seat and dozed off. Jaime drifted in and out of painkiller-induced sleep.

Peta watched him carefully while reading over the doctor's instructions. How cruel fate was, putting him so close within her reach yet making him still so unavailable. How many nights had she lain awake visualising the moment they would meet again? Except in her dreams, he'd swept her up in his arms, declared his undying love for her and demanded she marry him because he couldn't live without her.

How very different reality was from dreams. Now fate had thrown them together in close confines how would it end? Peta sighed. No matter what happened at the end of this fiasco, she would always love Jaime. There could never be any other.

She looked down at his sleeping face, leaned down and kissed his firm lips. Why not? She closed her eyes and savoured the feel of his lips against hers.

Seconds later her eyes flew open again as those lips moved under hers, capturing her mouth rather firmly for a man who was meant to be asleep. Startled green eyes met laughing, rich hazel ones, and she pulled back hastily.

'Taking advantage of an injured man, Peta? That's a bit unfair,' he muttered.

Peta buried her burning face in the doctor's notes. 'Checking to see if you're still breathing.'

Jaime chuckled, the deep sound sending delicious shivers down her spine. 'All you have to do is ask, honey, and I'll oblige. You don't have to wait until I'm asleep to steal kisses. It's far more enjoyable when I'm awake, you know.'

'Don't be a smart arse. Go back to sleep.'

'My pulse may be a bit erratic right now, nurse. And I'm pretty sure my blood pressure has skyrocketed.' He turned his head and laid it against the side of the seat, close to her shoulder, his gaze on hers. 'If we were alone and anywhere else but here, and if my body wasn't quite so sore, you would know exactly how I'm feeling about you, Peta. You're like a virus in my bloodstream I don't want to find a cure for.'

'First time I've been called a virus.' Peta's heart stuttered. 'And that's the pain meds talking.'

'Maybe, maybe not. We'll find out soon enough when we're alone.'

His eyes held a promise that warmed her cheeks. Peta shivered, but it wasn't fear that played on her spine and made her blood heat. There was something to be said for being put into isolation for a while. They would have a lot of time to explore their renewed feelings for one another while they waited for the bad guys to be caught. Jaime drifted off to sleep, and she couldn't stop a smile stretching her lips and hope lifting her heart.

Chapter Fifteen

After what seemed like a lifetime, but was probably less than a couple of hours, the light aircraft glided expertly to a stop on the runway of a small airfield. Harold unloaded bags from the chopper then helped Jaime onto the crutches and led them to a small hangar. Harold lifted the tarpaulin off a four-wheel drive parked in the corner and tossed the bags in the back.

'You've got a couple of weeks' worth of supplies in there. You should be right for a while.'

'Thanks, Harold. It looks like Mark has thought of everything.' How could she be angry with him when she knew he only meant well?

'Right, let's get you moving.'

Peta settled into the back seat with Bella while Harold helped Jaime into the front where he could stretch out his injured leg. Harold started the car and drove out the hangar to negotiate the rough terrain around them.

'Where are we?' Peta looked around. The landscape stretched ahead, deserted except for scattered bush, rough tracks and red dust.

'An out of service holiday resort. It used to be a railway siding many years ago until they re-purposed it. Unfortunately, not many people wanted to holiday out in the middle of nowhere. Suits our purpose though. You'll be staying in the owner's residence. It's furnished and we had someone come out to clean it and stock up the pantry with essentials,' Harold replied.

'What about you?' asked Peta.

'I have to go back. I'm not happy about leaving the three of you alone out here, but I have to respect Mark's orders.' Harold hesitated. 'You're like family to me, Peta. You've been through enough. I don't want to see you hurt.'

Jaime's laugh was grim. 'If that's a warning for me, big fella, you don't have to worry. I'll be on my best behaviour.'

'That's a given, Caruso, or I'll see you regret it for the rest of your life.'

'Point taken, mate.'

'Cut it out, you two.' Peta sighed. 'I can take care of myself. Will we be okay out here on our own, Harold?'

'Don't worry, it's perfectly safe here. No one even

knows this place still exists. You won't need my protection.' Harold looked at her. 'But I'll always have your back. Life seldom gives us a second chance, Peta. Take what you want if you want it. If it doesn't work, Jeannie and I will always be there to pick you up and dust you off. Just make sure it is what you want.'

Peta leaned forward and patted his shoulder. 'Thank you, Harold. I love that you care.'

'Only a fool would have let you go in the first place.' He cast a sideways glance at Jaime. 'Let's hope fools don't make the same mistake twice.'

Harold drew his eyes back to the road. He steered the vehicle off onto a side track and drove some way before reaching the boundary fence of a small compound. The whole place carried an abandoned air about it as they drove up the corrugated road. The concrete pool on the left an empty blue hole in the ground, plastic chairs upturned and yellowed by the sun, a red picnic umbrella still tied up and faded by degrees. On the right, cabins stood empty against the shimmering landscape, the dusty windows a reminder of holidays past. A little further ahead, they pulled up next to a small sandstone cottage with a faded red iron roof and a wraparound veranda that promised cool comfort within.

Outside the cottage the lawn grew knee-high, the garden beds overflowed with weeds and remnants of plants that hadn't survived the scorching summer heat. Inside however they were met by the clean, fresh smell of lemon, lavender and beeswax. On either side of the long hallway, two doors opened up onto bedrooms, a third to the bathroom and a fourth to a powder room. The end of the hallway spread out into a lounge room with an open plan kitchen and a one-eighty-degree view of sparse bushland from tall windows.

Harold dropped the last of the supplies inside the small hallway and then stood aside to let Jaime hobble in on his crutches. 'Well, I'll be off again. Feel free to explore, but don't wander outside of the compound. You're in the middle of the bush. It's easy to get lost out here.' He handed Peta a mobile phone. 'That's your only communication. Signal's not too bad out here but limited to hot spots. Don't forget to charge up the battery. There's a spare battery and charger in the cupboard over there.' He indicated to a small cabinet next to the television. 'We'll contact you as soon as we're certain it's safe for you to come home, but if you need us, just yell.' Harold hugged Peta and Bella before striding back to the door. 'Right, you're on your own. Caruso, take care.'

Jaime's eyebrow rose at the warning, but he nodded and replied, 'I will. Off you go now and don't worry about us. We'll be fine.'

Harold left with a wave for the girls and a hard look aimed at Jaime.

'For God's sake,' he muttered as the door closed behind Harold. 'I wouldn't dare put a foot wrong even if

I could.' Jaime moved closer to the sofa, each movement awkward and bringing a grimace to his face. 'It's good to know they're looking out for you.' He stood on his good leg and pulled the crutches out from under his arms then lowered himself down onto the sofa using them for balance.

Peta turned to take them from him as he sat. 'Okay?' She arranged cushions behind him and helped him lean back. The grey pallor of his face and the fine film of sweat on his forehead told its own story. 'I'll get you a couple of painkillers and then make us a bite to eat.'

'Good girl.' Jaime's hand tightened around hers. 'We need to talk.'

Peta pulled her hand from his. 'There's time enough for that, Jaime. You need to rest a little first. We'll be here a while.' She turned away, her hand on her chest, her fingers tingling from the feel of his skin against hers, her heart racing at the thought of the conversations to come and what they'd mean for them as a family.

She walked across to the kitchen and poured a glass of water from the sealed bottles she found in the fridge. Opening her handbag, she took out Jaime's prescription painkillers. They'd make him sleepy and delay any confrontation for later. It would give her time to get her thoughts together, especially being alone with him for an indefinite amount of time. With a muttered curse for the circumstances that had forced them into this situation, she walked back to where

Jaime rested his head against the back of the sofa, his eyes closed.

'Here we go.' Peta held out the painkillers and the water.

His eyes snapped open, dull with pain. She missed that teasing glint they used to carry. He eased forward to take them, wincing as he jarred his knee. Guilt that she was responsible for getting him shot, settled in her stomach like lead. The least she could do was help him heal physically. Emotionally, she and Bella would be the ones to suffer.

'You'll feel better after these.' She waited as he swallowed the pills and handed her back the glass. 'Bella, darling, can you stay with Jaime while I make us a snack? If he needs anything, you come and get me okay?' Bella shifted on her feet, looking uncertain. Peta ruffled her daughter's hair. 'What's the matter, sweetheart?'

'Mum? Is Jaime my dad?'

Peta's feet froze on the worn carpet. She looked at Jaime who shrugged. 'Why do you think that?'

'Because Paul said my real father was coming to find me when we were at that old house. He said that's why we had to hide. But Jaime isn't a bad man. Paul is. Jaime didn't lock me up or make me scared.'

Peta knelt down in front of her daughter, drawing her into a hug. 'We never have to hide from Jaime, Bella. He's a good man.'

'Is he my real dad?'

'Yes, Jaime is your real dad.'

'If he's a good man then why did he leave us?'

Damn good question and not one she wanted to have to explain to a child who had already experienced so much heartbreak. But then so much had happened in their lives that shouldn't have. 'Sometimes grownups make decisions they think are the right ones.'

'And sometimes they make big mistakes,' added Jaime, his voice laced with pain. 'Bella, honey, I would never do anything to frighten or hurt you. Not you or your mum. We have a lot to work out between us and I hope you will give me the chance to make it up to you, okay?'

Bella turned to Jaime, assessing him as she chewed her lip. Her little girl had been so brave all throughout her ordeal, even at the very last when she'd huddled in the corner terrified. All Peta wanted for her now was love and warmth and security that would erase those memories from her nightmares.

'Okay, but I have lots of questions.' Bella sat cross-legged on the carpet and looked up at him where he lay on the sofa.

'Sweetheart, Jaime needs to rest. He's in a lot of pain and needs to sleep to make him better. Can we save the questions for later?'

Jaime lifted his head and smiled. 'It's okay, Peta. Let her ask. It will take both our minds off things.'

Peta's heart did a quick dance. Paul had always been annoyed by Bella's questions. And injured, surely the last thing Jaime wanted to be doing was answering a little girl's questions. 'Are you sure?'

'We all have questions needing answers. It makes sense to answer them while we're here, away from civilisation. I'm not hiding from anything anymore.'

Finally, everything would be out in the open, all the questions answered, and then they could move forward. 'Okay then, if you're sure. But if you get too tired … please let her know when you've had enough.'

'We'll be fine.' And the look in his eyes promised they would be.

Leaving them together, she headed off to rummage in the supplies for the ingredients to make a light snack. Across the room Bella talked, her incessant questions barely pausing to give Jaime a chance to answer. He didn't seem too fussed by her chatter, a smile on his face as he listened.

Ten minutes later, she placed a plate of nachos in front of them. They ate in silence — Jaime already drowsy from the painkillers, Peta absorbed in her thoughts and Bella just plain hungry as she ate her share.

What would they say to one another once Bella wasn't there to act as a barrier? Her little girl couldn't take her eyes off Jaime, awestruck by his presence and the fact that she had a real flesh and blood dad, not a mythical creature who existed in a relayed memory. If he disappeared out of their lives now, Bella would be heartbroken.

Doubts niggled at Peta's mind. If Jaime was as afraid of commitment now as he had been back then, the chances of him hanging around were slim. The damage was already done. Bella had already fallen for him and the fire that burned in her own belly for the man she loved had not damped down. Children had the knack of bouncing back, but Peta wasn't sure her heart could survive another goodbye. She sighed heavily as she cleared away the empty plates and walked across to stack them in the kitchen sink.

'You think too much, Peta.' Jaime's drowsy voice interrupted her thoughts.

She turned, leaning back against the bench, her fingers curled around the edge of the wood. 'I have to. Someone has to.'

'We'll take care of this together, I promise you that.'

Promises were easy to make. Seeing them through was an entirely different ball game. 'That's a big responsibility, Jaime. Are you sure you're ready for it?'

Her question was met by Jaime's breathing. Her answer would be a while coming. He'd fallen asleep.

Chapter Sixteen

Jaime awoke to dimmed lights, flat on his back, stretched out on the sofa with a blanket across his legs and a pillow under his head. Outside the tall windows night had fallen across the barren landscape, the darkness pitch black. Muffled voices floated down the hallway from the bedroom. A drowsy smile touched his lips. He could get used to that. How nice it would be to have Bella and Peta there when he woke up every morning.

What? Jaime jerked up onto his elbows, wincing as white-hot pain seared down his leg. He grimaced and rubbed the bruised, bunched muscle in his thigh. For God's sake, he was thinking marriage, long-term, a lifetime.

A cold sweat formed on his brow. Fever or fear … more likely the latter. He couldn't let them walk out of his life, not now, not after everything they'd been through, but complete commitment? A whole different story. That meant sacrifice, changing the plans he'd had for his future, adapting them to accommodate a family — a wife and a daughter, maybe a new baby, a son.

He shoved a hand through his hair and chewed on his lip. It would be the right thing to do by Peta even if it was a few years too late, but would it be the best thing for his daughter? Was it Bella stirring up this need for commitment? So many marriages floundered because couples stayed together for the sake of the children. No, he loved Peta. He always had. He'd never stopped loving her.

The nagging voice in the back of his mind had his thoughts in turmoil. Jaime rubbed his eyes with the base of his palms. Too hard to think about with a mind fuzzy with painkillers. Gingerly, he lay back against his pillow again, closing his eyes. Time would tell. The door up the hallway closed and Peta's footsteps moved closer. He opened his eyes again as she stepped into the lounge room.

'Oh, you're awake. How are you feeling?'

'Better. Still sore,' he admitted, gritting his teeth.

'Well, it might be for a while. I'm so sorry, Jaime. If it wasn't for me you wouldn't be in this mess,' Peta apologised.

'As I've said before, I volunteered my services.

Please don't take the blame for what happened. Come, sit down and talk to me.'

Jaime levered himself up onto his elbows again, desperately trying to ignore the pain that shot through him as he did so. He hoped Paul Price was in ten times more agony because he sure as hell deserved to be.

'How's Bella doing?'

'She's doing okay. We've had a long chat. She's a little unsettled, but Paul had her in the old homestead right up until yesterday. Mark was right. He didn't harm her in any way. He was angry and gruff, but he fed her and mostly let her watch cartoons on television once he got the old generator going. No different really to when we lived with him.'

'What about the times he left her alone at night?'

'I'd say she would be sleeping already when he did. She said the only time she was scared was when he locked her in the shipping container. At least even there, he left a light on for her. Seems at odds with the violence he showed towards me.'

'His fight wasn't with her. She was just a means to an end, more valuable unharmed. And of no emotional value to him. Did he tell her why he took her away?'

Peta sat down on the floor next to the sofa, her arm on the cushion next to him. Warmth flooded him as her elbow bumped his thigh. Hastily she moved it away. He hated that she felt she needed to. It had been such a natural, comforting move and he liked having her close again. If he wasn't injured, he'd haul her up next to him and cuddle her into the curve of his body like old times.

'He told her he was sorry for being so mean to us, that he was taking her on a road trip to the town I was born in to make it better. That I'd be coming too, meeting them there. I guess he stuck as close to the truth as possible.'

'What about the drugs? He was pretty high when he ambushed us at the car.'

'He only took those once she was locked up. The high was only just kicking in. The scene at the old warehouse was set up. He never had her there at all. I can't tell you how grateful I was to hear that.' Hugging her knees to her chest, she leaned her head back against the seat cushion.

'He was messing with your head. Will she be okay sleeping alone in the room?'

Peta nodded. 'I've left the bedside lamp and the old clock radio on for her just in case. Once she's asleep, she's pretty good at staying that way. She's a tough kid.'

'Like her mum.' He touched her hair lightly, letting the soft weight fall through his fingers. 'I'm glad you didn't cut it.' He wound a length of it around his finger. The silkiness brought back memories of her hair spread out on his pillow or feathering across his chest after they'd made love. His body tightened in response. He could almost feel it now. He wanted to feel it again, but

Peta sat too stiffly at his side. If he kissed her, she'd resist. They had to bury the past first.

'Jaime, why didn't you tell me the truth when you went away?' she asked.

He sighed heavily. The time had come. There was no point in avoiding it any longer. 'I sent you a letter explaining everything.'

'What letter?' Peta turned to look at him, confusion evident in her frown.

'The letter I sent to say I'd joined the RAA. Don't you remember? You answered it.' Dread settled cold and heavy in his gut. Had she forgotten?

'I never got a letter from you, Jaime, never. How could I have answered a letter I never got?'

'What do you mean you never got it? Who answered it then?'

He turned to his side to look her right in the eye. Her eyes never lied. Peta had never been capable of telling a lie. He'd always loved that innocent honesty about her. 'Who answered the letter?' he asked again.

Peta stared up at him and he watched her face as realisation dawned.

'Mum.' Her hand came up to cover her eyes. 'It could only be Mum. I never saw the letter. I swear, Jaime. She must have recognised your writing and opened it. What did it say?'

'My letter or your reply?' It all made sense now.

Especially after Peta's mother had refused to let her speak to him when he'd called.

'My reply,' she whispered.

'In a nutshell, it said that you were glad I'd left, and I wasn't to bother you again.' He lifted another fall of hair and rubbed it between his fingers. 'Knowing you as I did, it didn't make sense at the time, but I figured you were angry. I stupidly accepted that you'd moved on. It's what I meant for you to do, even though I didn't want you to.'

Peta shook her head. 'How could you have believed that after everything we'd shared?' She groaned, covering her face with her hand. 'How could Mum do that to me?'

Jaime shrugged and lay back against the arm of the sofa. He placed an arm over tired eyes. 'She thought she was protecting you.'

'Protecting me? By sending me straight into the arms of someone like Paul? Yes, that was a good move, wasn't it?' Peta scoffed.

'Don't blame your mum. She loves you, Peta, and she only wanted what she thought was best for you. No-one knew what Paul was really like. Mark told me about him, even ran a background check on him to make sure he was legitimate, and he came up clean. No records, no misdemeanours, not even a lousy speeding ticket.'

'You knew about him?'

Jaime shrugged. 'Mark told me at the hotel in

Williams. Let's face it, we were too young. What we had between us was huge, it could have been so much more, but maybe the timing wasn't right.'

Peta turned and placed her chin on her arms against the cushion on the sofa. Her soft gaze on his had his blood warming rapidly, the pain in his thigh turning to a dull ache he could ignore if he could only hold her close again.

'And what about now, Jaime? Is there too much water under the bridge?'

Jaime sighed. Perhaps there was. They were older, wiser and even though she still set his body on fire, his heart needed convincing. 'I don't know. I am so confused right now. With seeing you again and finding out about Bella, I just don't know what I'm feeling.'

'What I don't want you to feel is obligation. You don't owe me anything,' Peta said, the warning in her voice clear. If he stayed, he had to prove he was there for the right reasons.

'So you keep telling me.' He turned his head to look at her, the need to hold her and draw comfort from her growing stronger every minute. 'Come up here and lie next to me.' He saw her hesitation as she moved away from the sofa. 'Just lie next to me, Peta, please. That's all I'm asking. I think we both need a little human contact.'

'I'm scared, Jaime,' she whispered.

'What are you scared of?' he whispered back.

'Of feeling too much.'

There was that brutal honesty again. Jaime tugged her closer. 'I never meant to hurt you and I promise I'll try not to do so again. I'm scared too, probably even more so than you.' He tugged a little harder until she gave in, climbed onto the sofa next to him and lay in the crook of his arm. With her head snuggled into his neck, he inhaled her scent. 'Bella does change things a little though.' Jaime felt her stiffen and move to pull away. He tightened his arm around her. 'Relax, don't get all defensive now. What I mean is I couldn't ignore her existence and go away quietly. You know that.'

Peta snuggled down again. 'I know that. That's why I swore Mark to secrecy about her existence.'

He hugged her closer. 'I'd like to be part of her life. Would that be a problem?' She stiffened against him, so he let his fingers drift along her spine, soothing the tension away until she relaxed again.

'I can't have you deciding down the track that it's all too hard and you leave us.'

The word *again* lay between them like a thorn under his skin. Jaime shook his head. 'If I make a commitment to her, it will be for life, I promise. If I fail, you can send Harold after me.'

'You can bet your life on that one.' She moved her head to look up at him and he met her gaze willingly. 'Don't let her down, Jaime.'

'I won't. That's a promise I intend to keep.'

'It's a start.'

She smiled and his heart did a belly flop to his stomach. He hadn't forgotten how sexy that smile was and the magic it could weave in his blood. Their lips were so close. If he moved forward a little, he could touch his mouth to hers. Just a little kiss, just one. His head moved towards hers. She met him halfway.

He feathered his lips across hers, teased her mouth until it parted. She kissed him back and the flame that had lain dormant inside him for so long ignited as she nibbled at his lip. Then his mouth possessed hers, deepening the kiss until he forgot where his soul started and hers ended. His mind screamed for him to stop but her fiery response overrode the warning, and he kissed her a little longer until his body ached with the need to possess hers.

He had to stop it now. There were things between them that needed to be fixed and this wasn't the way to fix them. Not if they wanted forever. Jaime pulled away slowly and placed a finger over the spot his lips had just left.

'Let's sleep on it. Tomorrow, things may be a bit clearer.' He pulled the blanket up over them, curled her into him and kissed her temple. 'Goodnight, Peta.'

Chapter Seventeen

Peta woke to the smell of frying bacon and eggs and subdued chatter. She stretched her cramped muscles, making a mental note to make it to a bed tonight. Sleeping on a sofa could be very uncomfortable when there were two of you. She listened as Jaime and Bella talked quietly, straining her ears to hear what they were discussing so seriously.

'So, what do I call you?' She heard Bella ask.

She cracked open her eyes to see Jaime smile at his daughter. 'Whatever you feel comfortable with.'

Bella studied him thoughtfully. 'I never called Paul 'Dad', you know. He never really took that much notice of me. He's very sick, Uncle Mark says. He doesn't mean to hurt us. He just can't help it.'

Jaime nodded. 'That's right, and where he is now they'll be able to help him get better.'

Bella looked up at him with a concerned frown. 'I won't have to see him again, will I? I know he didn't mean to hurt us, but I'm still frightened of him. I wouldn't like him to hurt my mum again either.'

'No, sweetheart, you don't have to see him again if you don't want to,' he comforted her.

'So can I call you Dad then?' she asked. 'Because you really are my dad, aren't you? We learn about those things in school, you know. Abby has a real dad, but Marcy has a step dad. Paul never really felt like a dad because he never did dad stuff with me.'

Peta's heart ached and she felt a prick of tears behind her eyes. Something so seemingly insignificant amongst everything else that had happened to them had made such a big impact on her baby. She hadn't given thought to the fact that the older Bella got, the more clearly she'd understand the difference her real father could make in her life. Peta blinked the tears away and blew out an unsteady breath, waiting for Jaime's response.

'It would make me very happy and proud if you did call me Dad, but we need to make sure that's okay with your mum first, okay?' He hugged Bella's tiny shoulders gently. 'We have a lot of catching up to do.'

She nodded thoughtfully, wise beyond her years. 'Okay. Mum says we have to give you space. She says if you love someone you need to give them the freedom to make up their own mind. But what happens if they make the wrong choice and go away instead?'

Jaime grimaced. 'Even adults make the wrong decisions sometimes. They think they're doing what's best for each other and then learn pretty quickly that they've made the wrong choice. Then they try to make it right again.'

'Did you make a mistake by not marrying my mum? Are you going to fix it now?' Bella asked him, eyes wide with innocence.

Jaime flushed and stammered. 'Umm … Bella, you know …' He ran a hand around the back of his neck. 'Marriage is … well … It takes two people to decide when to get married and to fix problems they're having. Your mum and I have a lot we need to sort through together. It's going to take some time, especially since we haven't seen each other for so long.'

Peta stifled a grin at seeing Jaime a little rattled. His answer seemed to satisfy Bella though because she gave him a bright smile and changed the subject.

'When do I get to meet my new nonna? I can speak a little Italian, you know,' she said proudly.

'I'm sure it will be very soon, Bella. She's going to be surprised to have such a clever granddaughter and will be very proud of you.' Jaime ruffled her hair.

Peta shivered. That was a hurdle they hadn't yet had time to consider. She prayed that they would accept these new developments with more grace this time around. Confrontations with his parents had seldom gone well, not when they'd held out hope that he would come to his senses and marry a good Italian girl.

Peta pushed away the blanket and rolled off the sofa to make her way towards the kitchen bench. 'Good morning,' she greeted cheerfully, kissing her daughter's cheek before hugging and tickling her skinny little body. Bella squirmed and giggled. A little unsure of how to greet Jaime, Peta settled onto a chair and grinned up at him. 'What's cooking? And should you even be standing on that leg?'

He grinned back at her. 'On today's menu we have bacon and eggs. And military boys are built tough. Sleep well?' His eyes darkened with mischief as a blush crept into her cheeks.

She lowered her eyes, embarrassment sparring for a position with frustration. Being so close to him all night had tested her resolve to keep her distance when all she wanted was to curl into him, skin on skin, and let him ease the years of loneliness. 'Yeah, okay. How's the leg feeling?'

'Sore. Numbed by painkillers, but I needed to move. The sofa was a bit too small,' he said, his eyes full of meaning as he looked at her. Jaime placed a plate of bacon and eggs on the bench top. 'Eat up. And you too, young lady,' he said as he handed Bella her share. 'You can stack the dishes in the dishwasher while your mum and I shower and dress.'

And didn't that raise a whole new scenario in her head of steamy water and soapy bodies sharing a shower stall. Peta held her breath and concentrated on Bella's response instead, expecting some resistance from her daughter who hated kitchen duties. To her surprise Bella said meekly, 'Sure, Dad, no problem.'

Peta looked at Jaime and raised her eyebrows. He shrugged. Bella looked at them curiously.

'Are you going to shower together?' she asked innocently. 'Because, you know, my friend Sandy's parents do. She told me they take a very long time in the shower, but it saves water.'

Peta choked on the coffee she'd just taken a sip of and coughed. Jaime laughed awkwardly, but the heated look he turned on Peta suggested he wouldn't be against the idea.

'Banish the thought.' Damn him for reading her mind. 'And we'll have to wrap that bandage in plastic wrap to stop it getting wet.'

He cleared his throat and scratched his head, adorably uncomfortable in the spot his daughter had put him on. 'No, Bella. I think it's safe to say we don't have to save water here. I'm sure your mum would like the bathroom to herself. Eat up now, Bell, there's a good girl.'

He bent across and tapped her little nose, such a sweet, fatherly thing to do that it hurt Peta's heart. Every day they spent together meant Bella would grow closer to Jaime, become more reliant on his presence and when the time came for him to leave, Peta would be left to pick up the pieces again. And this time it wouldn't only be *her* heart that would be broken.

Pushing her plate away, her appetite gone, she said, 'Should I try and ring Mark for an update?'

Jaime shrugged. 'I'm sure they'll let us know as soon as there are any new developments. Mark did say it could take time to make the arrests, maybe even a little longer than expected. We don't want to compromise our location by ringing in either. These days there are trackers in mobile phone satellites everywhere. It wouldn't take them long to find us if they really wanted to.'

Peta sighed. 'I just want it over and done with so we can all move on from this awful nightmare.'

Jaime placed his hand over hers and squeezed her fingers. 'I know. Closure,' he said. 'I think we all need it. We need to talk about us, Peta.'

They couldn't delay it any longer, not when the past lay between them and their daughter's future. 'I know,' she said. 'We'll talk about it tonight.'

'Tonight,' he agreed. 'Would you like to use the bathroom first? I'll help Bella clear away.'

Peta nodded and slipped off the chair. The time had come to lay the ghosts to rest. She should be happy about that. Instead, a hollow feeling settled in her stomach as she made her way to the bathroom, because the outcome still appeared bleak.

All through the morning, as she and Bella did a little weeding in the garden and Jaime rested his leg on a chair in the sun, Peta's thoughts churned over what had happened between her and Jaime. She tried to make sense of her mother's actions that sent him away, of his responses before he left and Mark's role in getting them back together again.

By late afternoon, her nerves were at breaking point and every look he sent her way made her want to run into his arms and beg him not to leave them again. Not when she'd fallen in love with him all over again. Not when she'd never stopped loving him, she just loved him differently to the way she had before.

The innocence of that youthful love was gone, but the foundation it had grown from remained, and she wanted to learn more about Jaime, the man he'd become rather than the man he'd been. Later they'd talk, unravel the tangled mess between them, find a solution to the challenges they faced. Peta wasn't sure what scared her the most. If he stayed or if he left.

Preparing the evening meal challenged her dexterity with him sitting across from her shirtless after a shower, his body contoured by muscle she wanted to feel under her palms, the tattoo of a bird in flight etched across his heart she wanted to trace with her fingertips. The grey that pain had etched into his features yesterday was gone, chased away by painkillers, the healing process, fresh air and sunshine. In its place, that devastating smile that turned her legs to jelly and her mind to mush. How could she ever have believed she'd get over him?

Night fell with inevitable darkness that matched her mood by the time Bella was tucked up in bed, the dishes were washed and packed away, and Jaime patted the seat next to him on the sofa. The moment she hadn't wanted to happen ever, yet ached to get over with now, had arrived. Either way, she'd be picking up the broken pieces of her heart.

'Look,' said Jaime, tugging on Peta's hand, threading his fingers through hers until she sat next to him, 'No matter how much I think it over, I come back to the same conclusion. Seeing you again, experiencing what you've been through … I want to make it up to you.'

'You don't owe us anything. If you want to do this because you feel you need to, that's the wrong reason to renew what we had.' She couldn't swallow past the lump in her throat, the sadness that weighed heavily in her chest.

His thumb drew circles against her pulse, sending spikes of pleasure through her bloodstream, melting the lump a little. 'I don't want what we had, sweetheart. I want what we could have. We're different people now to who we were back then. Older, wiser. We both know what we want now. I want to marry you. I want us to live together, raise our daughter as a family. The truth is, I have never loved anyone else but you.'

Her heart wanted to believe it was true, but her mind churned over the past, the obstacles and ghosts that still lurked at the edges of this reunion. 'What will your parents say? I can't see that their dreams for you will have changed. I was never their first choice for you, never will be.'

'Maybe not, but it's what I want for us. What I hope you want too. When we get back to town, we can go and see them together. Introduce them to their grandchild. They'll be stoked with her, Peta. She's a smart kid and a credit to your parenting skills.' He placed her hand on his good thigh, untangled his fingers from hers, put his arm around her shoulders and drew her against him until her head rested against his shoulder.

Peta sighed and snuggled into his embrace, the doubts still churning in her head but the warmth of his body taking the chill out of them. 'Are you sure, Jaime? Really, really sure that this is what you want? I can't bear to go through it all again. I've never stopped loving you and would give up everything I have to be with you so that we can be a family. But, down the track, if this isn't what you want, and it doesn't work out … I don't want you doing this for Bella's sake.' The thought of losing him again had her stomach in knots.

'Let's be a family. It's what we need to be. What we

should have been,' Jaime said, clasping her chin in his hand and turning her face up to his.

She met his lips halfway, his kiss so tender and sweet it made her eyes sting with tears. 'A compromise,' she said, a breath away from his tantalising mouth.

He raised an eyebrow. 'A compromise?'

Peta nodded. 'We'll take this one step at a time.'

'Deal,' said Jaime, his mouth a whisper above hers. 'Can we seal the deal? Because I really need to kiss you again.'

And more than anything in the world, she needed to taste his lips on hers, the promise they held, the future they showed. 'Deal,' said Peta, drawing his head down to hers and closing the distance.

Jaime kissed her, his hands leading a trail of magic along her legs, the warm feel of his skin against hers sending shivers through her, driving a desperate need to have him naked next to her. Nothing had changed. The thought of them together, side by side, skin on skin, it was all she needed to be whole again.

Those hands, so warm and strong, worked their way up her thighs leaving a trail of need in their wake. His palm cupped her bottom, stroked the skin as he eased her down until they lay side by side. Bodies aligned, every curve of his pressed against hers, she felt him, hard and wanting. Her hands worked their way through his hair and back down around to cup his face, slightly rough from a day's growth of beard. Every touch of his skin against her palms made her hungry for more of him. Ten years was too long. Too long not to have him with her every night, not to feel the press of his body against hers, not to have him fill every inch of her body with the love and passion that had come so easily to them so long ago.

Was it too soon to say the words? Would it shatter the magic that had only just begun to blossom again? Would they come back to haunt her again? For a lifetime this time? 'I love you, Jaime Caruso,' she whispered, arching as his hand stroked across her belly. She ran her hands across his shoulders and down his muscled back, rediscovering every dip and rise, pressing him even closer until she felt she could crawl into him and stay there in the haven of his arms forever.

'I love you, baby. Always have, always will,' he whispered back. His clever fingers worked the buttons of her shirt loose, his breath hitching in his throat and releasing on a sigh when it parted to reveal she hadn't bothered with a bra. 'Beautiful,' he whispered and wasted no time showing her how much he adored her breasts.

Peta fisted her hands into his shirt, arching up against him, anchoring her legs around his, careful not to hurt his thigh. 'This needs to go,' she muttered, pushing the material up between them.

'Maybe we should take this into the bedroom in case

Bella wakes up and comes wandering through,' Jaime suggested, pushing himself up.

No. If they moved now, the dynamic would change. She'd lose him, the warmth he promised, the satisfaction she knew would be there at the end, the chance to make this real again. She closed her eyes, frowned against the panic that rose in her belly.

His thumb stroked across her lips, up to ease the crease from her forehead. 'It's okay, baby. Please don't be afraid of what we have, what we will have. I'll be more comfortable in the bed. This sofa wasn't made for making out with a bullet wound in the thigh.'

His tender smile eased the panic but made her realise the selfishness of her wanting him to the point that she'd forgotten his injuries. 'Oh God, Jaime, I'm sorry. Your leg—'

'Will be just fine, baby. Come, let's go to bed.'

'Yes,' said Peta.

She eased into the spot against his side, his arm draped around her shoulders, and they made slow progress up the hallway. Each step bringing them closer, each movement of their bodies against one another feeding the fire that grew inside her.

She closed the door behind them, releasing her hold on Jaime. He sat on the edge of the bed. For a split second, she hesitated, her hands pressed against the wood of the closed door. If she went through with this, there'd be no turning back. He eased his polo shirt over his head and in the light of the bedside lamp, the muscles in his torso rippled. He'd changed over the years, become harder, stronger. He'd been ripped then but now he had added maturity that made her hands itch wanting to explore the changes, rediscover the man who was the same yet different.

Then his gaze met hers across the room, eyes rich and warm, filled with an invitation to guilty pleasures. Ones she didn't deserve to have when her life lay in tatters around her, when the man who'd destroyed her life was still a threat and the one she loved was only a few steps away.

But then he eased himself out of his track pants, and she remembered how much she loved his strong thighs, sculpted from years on the local football team and maintained by his love of running. The only thing marring the beauty of everything that was Jaime Caruso, was the bandage that covered the skin where her ex-husband had shot him. She leaned her head back against the door, tears clogging her throat. She didn't deserve him. She should let him go. The danger wasn't over yet. What if Paul sent his thugs after them?

The track pants fell to the floor on top of his shirt, followed by his socks. Jaime's feet. Strong, big, broad and ticklish. She smiled at the memory of the times she'd taken advantage of that weakness until he'd been helpless under her hands and ready to give her anything she wanted. And she wanted him. Then, now and always.

'I can hear you thinking, baby. Come here.'

She pushed away from the door, crossing the room on shaky legs. He patted the spot on the mattress next to him. She sat, her eyes on his legs, her hands clenched in her lap. His arm came around her, across her back, his palm drawing relaxing circles on her hip. His lips found her temple and her lids fluttered closed at the warm sensation of his mouth on her skin.

His other hand worked her fingers out of the knot they were in, splayed them across those muscles in his thigh. They twitched underneath her hand, so she stroked them, her palms flat against the warmth, moving from muscle memory buried deep inside her mind. Her hands remembered him, her mind provided the pictures, and her blood was on fire for him once more. Gently he pressed her down to the bed, his body following hers slowly, gingerly.

'Your leg ...' She trailed her fingers across his ribcage, flattened her palm against his side.

'Will feel a lot better if we think of something else,' he whispered against her mouth, his hands busy as he loosened the button on her jeans and pulled down the zipper.

'Be gentle with me.' She pressed her hand against his as his fingers trailed the line of her underwear. Like the night they'd first been together this way. When making love had been a journey of discovery, each touch unearthing a new sensation, a newly discovered place of pleasure.

'Always.'

She lifted her hips, and he eased the denims down her legs, dropping them to the floor, her underwear following them down. All barriers removed, they lay savouring the feel of bare skin against one another, heated yet cool, eager yet patient, their hands and feet exploring, stroking, entangling.

The strength of his need pressed against her thigh, hard and seeking. She reached for him, her fingers running the length of him, her lips spreading in a smile as he murmured what he wanted in her ear. Then he lowered his head, took her mouth, nibbled at her lip, stroked her tongue with his, driving her crazy with teasing, making her want to devour his mouth and his body with a heated desperation before she reminded herself to slow it down.

Through the fog of desire, the tinny, electronic sound of ringing reached her ears. Jaime groaned and muttered something about lousy timing. 'I bet that's your bloody brother.'

'His timing has never been great. It's what makes him a good cop. He catches his suspects unawares.' Peta reached out to retrieve it from the bedside table and pressed the answer button. 'Hello?' she said, trying to keep a steady voice as Jaime's hands continued to work their magic.

'I hope I'm not interrupting anything,' Mark's voice replied in her ear.

Peta laughed, slightly breathless, as Jaime's hands stroked across her abdomen, trailed by his lips. 'No, of course not,' she squeaked, grabbing a fistful of Jaime's hair and halting his mouth as it approached its final destination. He blew out a warm breath at the apex of her thighs and she bit off a groan of pleasure.

Jaime grinned mischievously up at her before trailing his body up hers to plant a smacking kiss on her lips. Then he pulled the phone from her nerveless fingers, tapped the speaker icon and said, 'Make it fast, boyo. We're in the middle of negotiations here.'

Mark laughed loudly, his voice echoing through the speaker. 'Is that what they're calling it these days? Look, just calling in to say we've wrapped it all up into a tidy parcel on our side. Price sang like the bloody canary he is.'

'What about the threat to Peta?'

Peta stiffened under him, her breath hitching in her throat. He stroked her hair with gentle hands, soothing the tension from her body.

Mark's words almost had her tensing again. 'Their attentions have been turned elsewhere. Apparently they have a little trouble on the east coast they need to take care of involving a scandal with money laundering through a car dealership. Someone named Serena Snow is a far bigger threat to their organisation than Peta is. We're working on it with the cops in Sydney. They'll have to rethink their strategies. The evidence we gave Paul was passed to one of the runners in the Tag Raiders gang and never made it to Beyond Hell's Reach clubhouse. Tiny Watts' safety is our priority now. Albero and Bennetti won't think twice about silencing their lambs for good. No one misses the street kids.'

Peta wriggled under Jaime, desperate to get up as the horror of what Paul's associates were capable of began to kill off the passion she'd felt only moments earlier. Jaime shook his head and cupped her face. *Stay.* His lips formed the words silently, his arm anchoring her to him. 'Then you'd better get on with the job before anyone else goes missing.'

'Yeah, I'm on it.'

The seriousness in her brother's tone made her heart ache. He cared. Too much. More than he needed to. More than he should. She frowned.

Jaime smoothed the lines away. 'Mate, are you trying to kill the mood here?'

'What? No! No, not at all. Not ever. You have a mood going? That's great!'

Peta groaned against his side. Mark would never let her live this one down, but at least it put a happy note back in his voice. Jaime chuckled, the sound rumbling in his chest. He squeezed the hand she'd placed over the tattoo on his heart.

'Well, wrap it up then, mate.'

'Right. Wrap it up. Hope you're wrapping it up.' Mark chuckled. 'You guys can come home now. Unless, of course, you'd like a few more days in your deserted paradise, you know, to complete the … ahh … negotiation process?'

Jaime looked down at Peta and for a split second, she considered it. It would be nice to stay here tucked away from reality, but there were bridges to mend and the sooner they did so, the sooner they could settle things between them. She shook her head and Jaime sighed.

'When did you want to come and pick us up?'

'We'll fly in tomorrow morning at about eleven.'

'We'll be ready,' said Jaime.

'Hey, Caruso …'

'Yeah?'

'Take care of my sister.'

Jaime smiled down at her, promise in his eyes, and Peta's heart dipped and danced.

'Absolutely. Forever this time.'

'Yes! Harold, you owe me a beer.'

Mark's shout made Peta wince as it echoed around them before Jaime hit the end call button and tossed the phone on top of the pile of clothing.

'Now, where were we?'

Chapter Eighteen

Mark and Harold arrived dead on time and Peta was glad she'd eased out of bed at the crack of dawn to pack. It had been a tough decision to make in the cold, hard light of day when she'd spent the night in Jaime's arms relearning every inch of his body and falling in love with him all over again.

He'd lain there against the pillows, fast asleep, the shadow of a beard caressing his jaw, a pillow elevating his injured knee, an arm thrown out over his head. She'd wasted a few precious packing minutes just looking at him, remembering the hours they'd spent exploring each other, the number of times they'd turned to each other in the night.

So perfect. Almost too perfect. Despite the comfortable aura that had settled around them, the glances between them that were tender and new again, an uncomfortable churn settled in the pit of her stomach.

She met Mark's knowing smile with the pang it brought to her heart. Perhaps one day when the time was right, he'd have what they had. He'd find that special someone who made him feel alive again. He too could move on from playing rescue hero for her and find his own damsel to save.

Bella chatted happily to her uncle, her ordeal a weakening memory, slowly erased by life moving on. Soon she'd forget the terror she'd been through, and if their future with Jaime was as bright as it looked, she'd eventually forget it completely.

Jaime was clearly on the road to recovery, his colour normal again and, other than the need for crutches when he walked further than to the bathroom, there was little indication that he'd suffered an injury.

Peta smiled. When she'd looked in the mirror this morning, she'd noticed the shadows under her eyes had gone at last and she prayed with all her heart that they stayed away now that she'd found happiness in Jaime's arms again. Still the churn in her stomach niggled. They still had hurdles to overcome, perhaps their worst battle was still to come when they faced Jaime's parents, her mum, the people who'd kept them apart.

Harold herded them all into the small plane and settled himself in the pilot's seat. The plane rumbled down the short, dusty airstrip before the nose rose in the air and the resort became an unknown mark on the map once more.

Jaime's hand settled over hers in her lap, his fingers threading with hers, palm against palm. Peta tried hard to push back the niggling feeling that refused to settle in her belly. They were going to be okay. They could do this. They could face the past and lay the doubts to rest.

On arrival at Williams' rural air strip, Harold offered to drop Peta and Bella back to the hotel, while Mark drove Jaime home to his parents' house. She'd rather not leave his side. If he didn't come back …

'I'll see you later tonight,' Jaime told Peta with a kiss on the cheek and a comforting hand on her shoulder. He'd always had the uncanny knack of reading her doubt. 'We'll grab a bite to eat first before we go and see the parents.'

He bent down to give Bella a hug before he stood to meet her eyes, holding her gaze, promising without words. He'd promised before and then he'd disappeared. Could she trust him any more now than she had then?

'Six o' clock.'

'Okay,' she said and watched as he got into Mark's car, and they drove away.

They'd agreed it would be best to get the reunion with his parents out of the way as soon as possible. There'd been no reason to delay it any longer, but that didn't make Peta feel any less terrified. She doubted they'd feel any differently about her after all this time, not even with the presence of their grandchild. If they broke her little girl's heart or rejected her after all this time …

She wouldn't stand for that. She'd walk away. If they accepted Bella and not her? She'd deal with it out of fairness to Jaime. She'd let him go if they demanded it, but what would that do to her child? Family pressure was a passion killer, no matter what the outcome of this reunion.

'Come on, Peta, let's get you back to the hotel,' Harold urged, as she stared after the departing car. 'Is everything okay?'

Peta nodded and smiled up at him. 'Everything will work out as it's meant to,' she replied. 'Thanks, Harold, for everything you've done for us. It feels so good to have things back to normal again. Is Paul really safely away?'

'Yes, and he will be for a very long time. We've got him on some serious charges. Some his bent lawyers, Albero and Bennetti, might get him off on, others they won't. But trust me when I say, our eyes are on everyone in contact with Paul Price. He's not wiggling on our watch. There's no space,' Harold answered. 'About Caruso …'

Peta sighed. 'Let it go, Harold. If it works out, all well and good. If it doesn't, we'll deal with it when the time comes. We've come to an agreement to take it one step at a time. That's all I can ask.'

'You know I'll always be there for you, Peta, you only need to say the word. Jeannie too.' He put the car into gear.

Scrubbed, polished and dressed in her best outfit, Bella twisted in front of the mirror, admiring herself. 'Do I look pretty, Mum? Will Nonna and Nonno love me?'

'Of course they will, darling. You're beautiful.'

Peta carefully selected a trim pants suit in pale peach with a darker shade camisole under the jacket from her wardrobe. She matched it with strappy gold sandals. Earlier she and Bella had treated their toe nails to a delicate shade of varnish to match their outfits. Satisfied, she fastened a simple string of pearls around her neck and a heavy gold bracelet on her wrist to match her watch. Matching pearl earrings dangled from her ears on a short gold chain. She'd brushed her hair until it shone rich and full — bodied under the lights.

'You're going to knock their socks off, Mum,' said Bella. 'You look like a princess.'

Peta bent down and hugged her tightly. 'So do you, beautiful.'

A knock sounded at the door of the suite. 'That'll be Daddy,' yelled Bella as she ran to open the door. She let out a whoop as Jaime scooped her up and planted a loud kiss on her cheek.

'Well, look, I got me a little princess,' he said before putting her back on her feet and looking at Peta. 'Oh, and a fairy queen.' With Bella's hand still in his, they walked over to where Peta stood. 'My God, you're beautiful.'

'Thank you,' said Peta, a flush burning in her cheeks. She wanted to be beautiful for Jaime, every day, forever. Jaime leaned down and gave her a kiss that made her want to forget all about the meeting with his parents and stay home cuddled in bed with him instead.

'They'll love you both,' he said. 'Stop worrying.'

'How can you be so sure?' she whispered.

'I love you and that's all that matters.' He stroked her cheek with his finger, a reassuring touch that turned her knees to jelly. 'Come, let's go. Dinner is waiting in the dining room.' Jaime held out an arm to each of them.

Dinner was a happy affair and Peta wanted it to last forever. Even Jaime's confidence and show of commitment couldn't erase the feeling in her stomach that it wasn't going to be as easy as he made it sound. Her intuition had seldom failed her in the past.

A few minutes later, Jaime pulled up in front of his parents' home. Peta eyed the big double oak doors apprehensively. Her palms were sweaty, and she wiped them against the black upholstery of the seat. Jaime reached across to reassure her with a pat on her thigh. A little higher and she'd be happy to forget all about meeting his parents again.

'We're in this together now. They can't come between us again, Peta. This time I won't let them,' Jaime promised quietly.

Peta looked at him, doubts vying for attention in her mind, churning up her nerves. 'They did once before, quite easily. What if we're rushing things, Jaime? Maybe it's too soon. We're still raw from all that's happened in these last few days. Maybe we're being ruled by our emotions and not our heads. Maybe we should give it more time.'

Jaime shook his head. 'What happened between us last night was not a playback from the past, Peta. It was real and the feelings we have for each other are stronger than ever before. Please don't deny that,' he said as he saw her mouth move to interrupt. 'Don't get cold feet on me now. Let's just play it one day at a time, just like we planned. We've had a tough few days and a lot of changes. This time we have to see it through together. No more running away.'

Peta sighed and nodded. He was right. They had wasted enough time waiting for this to happen, expecting to have to deal with all the hurt some day. It had to be for real this time. It was their last chance granted to them by fate and her wonderful big brother. She owed it to Mark to give it her best shot, for everything he'd done for her, for them.

Jaime leaned over and kissed her. She returned his

kiss as if it were her lifeline, reluctant to let him go and face the ghosts.

'Oh yuck. Stop it, you two,' their daughter exclaimed from the backseat, loosening her seatbelt and placing her hand on the door handle. 'Let's go meet my nonna.'

Jaime pulled away with a sigh. Taking a deep breath, he looked at Peta, his eyes filled with promise and climbed out of the car. He helped them out onto the pavement, but didn't let go of their hands. 'Let's get this show on the road,' he muttered.

They walked up the long pathway to the front door, each step heavier than the last. The churning in Peta's stomach intensified, apprehension tugging at her throat and doubt lingering in the shadows of her mind.

Reaching the door, Jaime kissed them both. 'Whatever happens …'

Peta squeezed his hand before he let it go to reach for the door handle.

A tall, dark-haired woman threw open the door, her arms wide. 'Jaime, *tesoro*, where have you been?' she demanded, throwing herself into his arms. Jaime steadied himself with his hands on the woman's hips, wincing as his injured leg twisted under her weight. She hurried along in a spate of Italian, her hands all over his face, her lips smothering his cheeks in kisses, aiming for his lips.

Peta studied the woman carefully, the churning in

her stomach morphing into a full-blown tsunami. She was tall and willowy, about the same height as Jaime and the way she pressed her body to his indicated he knew her well. Very well. Her long, black hair was shiny and pulled back into a knot, tied with a red silk scarf. Her matching red suit screamed Armani. It took her a while to acknowledge her audience. And when she did, her eyes were filled with a spiteful possessiveness that threw ice-cold anger down Peta's spine.

'I'm sorry,' she said sweetly in a heavily accented voice. 'This man of mine just disappeared ... how do you say in English ... without a word to anyone.'

Peta's stomach curled into a tight knot as doubt edged back into her thoughts, stronger than before. The woman managed English perfectly well and she hadn't misinterpreted the situation. She'd made it perfectly clear. Jaime wasn't hers to keep. He belonged to another woman. And he'd done to her what he'd done to Peta. Had a case of cold feet.

She looked at Jaime, his jaw set, his lips pulled into a grim line and his hands still firmly on the woman's hips, knuckles white.

'Man of yours?' She hated the tremor in her voice, the way her throat tightened, and tears stung her eyes. The past rolled in to torment her again. The echo of his mother's voice in her head telling her about the girl from Tuscany he would eventually marry and bring together the two oldest families from the valley.

The girl raised her eyes heavenward. 'Yes,' she said impatiently as if Peta was a child who could not understand what she was saying. 'I am Maria, his fiancée.'

Peta felt her heart shatter, shards of glass that pierced every corner of her soul as they ripped her dreams to pieces and left them broken on the pavement outside his parents' house. Again. His fiancée? She looked at Jaime waiting for him to deny it, but he seemed to be at a loss for words. He stared at the woman in front of him as if she were a ghost.

'It seems there's something you've forgotten to tell me, Jaime,' she prompted, fighting back the tears that burned in her throat, looking to him to deny it, struggling to understand why he couldn't.

Jaime blinked and pushed the woman away, dropping his hands from her hips. Maria wasn't about to let go easily. She curled her hands possessively around his arm and stuck to his side like a tube of glue as she looked down at Peta, her perfectly shaped red lips parted in an ugly sneer.

Jaime tried to shake off the woman's hands, but his mouth remained closed on the words she wanted to hear. Maria chattered to him as if she and Bella weren't standing on the pavement with their dreams broken at their feet. He answered her in short, sharp words, none of them in English or aimed at Peta in an explanation. They were all for Maria.

'I think the situation explains itself.' Peta took Bella's hand, the little girl's fingers trembling in hers. How would she even begin to explain this to her daughter? Not when she'd only just found her father. Was that the plan all along? That Maria would make the perfect stepmother for Bella? Was all that had happened between them since they'd found each other again just another lie, another game he'd played with her?

'Goodbye, Jaime. I hope you and your … fiancée … are very happy together.' She turned away from them, the road ahead empty, her heart in her throat and tears burning behind her eyes because she refused to cry them for him. She began to walk, but Bella dug her heels in and brought her to a halt.

'Peta, wait,' Jaime called out, before turning angrily on the woman next to him.

Bella looked up at her mother, confused. 'Mum! Where are we going? Who was that horrible lady? Mum! Dad's calling you!' Bella pulled at Peta's hand.

'Not now, honey, we need to get back to the hotel,' she said, urging her daughter to walk, hurrying down the street, her calf muscles aching thanks to the high heels on her sandals.

She looked back at Jaime and Maria, and wished she hadn't. In the doorway, stood Jaime's mother, her hands clasped to her chest, words of happiness flowing over the couple, her satisfaction at seeing them together evident, and so complete she didn't need to glance down the street and see the pathetic figures they made — her and Bella — running away.

'Stop, Mum! I want my dad,' Bella begged, her little voice tearful.

Peta stopped and knelt down in front of her daughter. 'Dad has something he needs to sort out, Bella. Something he forgot to tell us about. When he's done sorting it out, hopefully he'll come and explain it to you.' Her voice was thick with emotion and unshed tears. She hoped he would, couldn't bear to think of the pain they'd suffer again if he didn't. Gently, she hugged her little girl. All they had left was each other. 'We'll be fine, you'll see.'

Bella looked at her, her bottom lip quivering, shattering the last piece of Peta's heart. 'He's going away again, isn't he? He's never going to be my dad.'

Her head began to pound from the tears she kept in check. It took all the control she possessed not to cry herself. Her gut instinct, as always, had been painfully correct. When would she learn to trust it? And all she had left to give her daughter, after all they'd been through with Paul, was the honesty that would break her heart.

'We have to wait and see, Bella, but yes, I think that's quite possible. Come on, let's go and ring Uncle Mark and get him to take us home to Grandma.'

'I don't want to go home to Grandma. I want my

dad. She's lying, Mum. He belongs to us now,' Bella cried, stamping her foot.

'Bella, stop that right now!' Peta took her daughter's shoulders firmly. 'He doesn't belong to anybody. Remember what I said about people being free to choose? Well, your dad has made his choice. Sweetheart, we have been through a lot over the last few weeks. So much has happened to us. So much has changed. We need time to settle down. Right now, though, we are going home.'

Her voice held a tone of finality Bella knew better than to argue against and she hated using it, but the walls needed to be rebuilt and life had to go on, even if that meant her soul had to die on Prospect Street in Williams.

Peta stood up, took Bella's hand once more and walked briskly in the direction of the hotel, thanking the gods that Williams was a small town, and that Prospect Street was so close to Main. Her mobile phone rang. She ignored it as she pushed through the hotel doors.

Inside their room, she threw their belongings into suitcases, mentally cursing Jaime for once again destroying her dreams. The room telephone rang, the sound shrill in the heavy silence. Peta ignored it. When it stopped, she rang the number for the reception desk and asked the girl on duty to hold all calls. Finally, she finished packing and rang Mark.

'Mark,' she choked around the lump in her throat.

'It's Peta. Can you come to the hotel please?' Her voice cracked on the words.

'Peta, what's wrong? Where's Jaime?' His tone swung from concerned to annoyed. His feelers would be out, his instincts on high alert. He'd had this call from her before.

'He's otherwise engaged.' She laughed bitterly at the unintended pun.

'I'll be over right away.' The line went dead in her ear.

Several minutes later he was knocking at her door, Harold hot on his heels. Peta gave them a watery smile, her gallant rescue team. They had always been there for her when she needed them, and today was no exception.

'Why did I believe him? Why didn't you leave it alone?'

Mark put his arm around her and hugged her close. 'I'm sure there's a perfectly good explanation for all this, Peta.'

Harold was not quite so sympathetic, already making plans to separate Jaime's head from his shoulders and being quite colourful about it too.

Peta shook her head. 'It doesn't matter. I just want to go home and put all this behind us. It was a mistake to think we could ever be together again. There's far too much water under the bridge. Jaime's actions were obviously guided by his sense of duty, just as I knew they would be when he found out about Bella.'

'No, Peta, that's not true. I've known Jaime a long time. I'm not mistaken about his feelings for you. Jaime loves you. He always has and always will. This thing between the two of you has eaten away at him. That's why he's still single,' Mark reassured her.

'That's where you're mistaken. He's not, is he? We have just seen his fiancée in the flesh, and he certainly didn't deny it. His mother was happy, no doubt about that. I saw it, heard it, don't need any confirmation. The truth never lies. I'll always be an outsider to his family.'

Mark shook his head. 'There has to be an explanation for all this. I was so sure …'

'Leave it alone. Your intentions were good, but your plan backfired. It's over.' Peta's tone brooked no further argument. The subject was closed. 'Take me home now, please.'

Mark sighed heavily. 'Okay, let's go. But I'm sure you're making a mistake.'

'He's your friend. Of course you'd think that.'

Mark picked up her luggage and Harold opened the door. 'I'll let that one go to the keeper, honey, because I know you're hurting right now.' He led the way down the stairs to the car and loaded it up.

As they began the two-hour drive through the bush-lined, winding roads back down to Perth, Peta looked back at Williams, nestled in the dust behind them and said goodbye to it forever. Certain this time she'd never return. Huddled in her corner on the back seat with her daughter against her side, she cried for what might have been.

'Jaime has a lot to answer for,' Mark decided. He glanced over his shoulder then back at Harold who steered the car through the dark country roads. 'I'll get to the bottom of this,' he promised.

Peta shook her head. 'I told you to leave it alone, Mark. You've got to let it go. Bella and I have all we need. Thank you for what you tried to do. I do love Jaime and probably always will, but our lives have taken different paths. We've grown up. What we had was puppy love and now it's over.'

'That's where you're wrong, Peta. You and Jaime are meant for each other. Look I don't know who this bird is, but if she really is his fiancée, don't you think I'd be the first to know? When I heard Jaime was going to be in town at the same time as us, I knew it would be the perfect opportunity to get you two together again, where you belong. He has been torn to pieces over you, Peta, trying to do the right thing by you. I figured some pushing wouldn't do any harm and that's why I arranged the whole bush dance thing.' Mark ran a frustrated hand through his hair.

'You always think your plans are foolproof.' Peta grimaced. 'You're a lousy matchmaker, Mark, but as best friends and big brothers go, you do all right.'

'Not a bad knight in shining armour either.' He tried to make her smile.

Peta sniffed and wiped away a tear. 'Why me, Mark? Haven't I endured enough? I get given hope and then get it taken away again.' She looked at him, anguish and disappointment squeezing her heart. 'I've delivered a baby, recovered from a nervous breakdown, conquered anorexia, raised a child, been beaten, stabbed and shot at, and now lost the man I love not once but twice. What am I doing wrong?'

'You are the most special person I know, honey. Not many people could have coped with what you have. But you did. This is just a small hitch. We'll get through it together just as we have every other challenge sent our way. We've batted all the curve balls and still made it home. This one won't be any different.'

She gave him a watery smile. 'Where would I be without you, Mark? Why didn't I fall in love with someone less complicated?'

Mark threw his hands up in the air. 'God forbid, I'd be out of a job then. The truth is,' he continued seriously, 'I think you should have stuck around to hear what Jaime had to say. You need to trust him, Peta. Give him a chance to explain. If he does want to explain, will you let him? Please?'

'He wasn't exactly tripping over his explanations tonight, Mark. In fact, his mouth was stitched tighter than the wound on his leg. This is what his family want for him. I can never be the perfect Italian wife.' She already knew it was over. Jaime would not come back a third time. He couldn't dispose of a fiancée that easily.

Three hours after he'd shaken Maria from his arm and told his mother in no uncertain terms the trouble she'd caused, Jaime nursed a drink at the bar of the Williams Hotel. Peta was gone.

The uneasy silence shattered as Harold crashed through the tables. He grabbed Jaime's arm and dragged him off the bar chair; a loud, angry wall of steel, his voice commanding the attention of all twenty-something patrons who looked ready to throw their hands in and help. Not even a decorated war veteran could get away with messing with the town's golden girl. Not then, not now, never. And he'd take what they dealt out and wear it.

'I warned you, Caruso. I should beat you within an inch of your life, you dirt bag. What do you think you're trying to prove?' Harold stood right in his face and Jaime didn't even try to fight back.

A glance to his right and he saw Mark moving quickly towards them. Mark grabbed Harold's shoulder. 'Hold it, mate,' he said. 'If anyone's going to punch him, I have first option. I'm off duty, you're not. Settle down, before you're up for police brutality.'

Harold growled angrily and gave Jaime a hard push before releasing his iron grip. Damn it, now his arm throbbed in time with his leg.

Mark patted Harold's back and pulled out a chair for him. 'Show's over, folks.' He watched the crowd disperse. 'Now, let's have a drink and figure this thing out.'

Harold lowered himself into the chair, reluctance in every move, making sure Jaime sat first under a glower that would make a prize-fighter proud. The barman placed their drinks in front of them and beat a hasty retreat.

Mark turned to Jaime. 'What's going on, Jaime? Who is this fiancée and why don't I know about her?'

Jaime sighed and took a healthy swig of his beer. He glanced warily at Harold who snarled at him in return. 'I thought I'd made it clear to everyone, then and now, that I wasn't interested in marrying Maria Ferraro. I never thought she would have the gall to come out here. Her parents and mine decided that Maria would make the perfect wife for me. They threw us together at every possible opportunity. Maria was over the moon, of course. The status that comes with being the wife of a possible mining magnate is too big to pass up. Despite the fact that I showed a deliberate lack of interest in the woman, she stuck like glue. I just couldn't shake her and the woman I did want to marry was far too young to be tied to me. So, I joined the military and went to Afghanistan to shake them both.'

'And what, she just happened to be in town?' Harold's snort earned him a warning look from Mark.

Jaime ignored him. 'I told my parents to back off or they would never see me again. I tried to explain to Maria that I wasn't interested in any sort of relationship with her. Unfortunately, she doesn't know how to take a hint and almost certainly doesn't take no for an answer. And yes, Harold, when I didn't travel to Italy as soon as I received my discharge, she hopped on a plane to come and find me. She told my mother that I'd proposed to her, and we were getting married now that I was back in civilian life. My mother was rapt, as you can imagine. And all this was happening while we were out of town with Peta's situation. By the time we got around to my mother's when it was all over, Maria had the whole scene set and Mum had the wedding all planned out.'

Harold looked at him in disbelief. 'You seriously want us to believe that shit? What time zone do you think this is? 1936?'

'It's the truth. When Peta and I arrived at the house, she was there. In her true flair for drama, she threw herself into my arms as if that was her rightful place to be. It was a pretty convincing act.' He smiled derisively. 'Anyway, by the time I'd gathered my wits, Peta was halfway down the road, and I couldn't chase her because my bloody leg had gone into a spasm. She won't answer my calls. Where is she? I went up to her room, but it was empty.'

Harold muttered some colourful words. Mark grinned and patted his shoulder. Looking at Jaime he asked, 'Would you have understood? Put yourself in her shoes, mate. If Maria was as convincing as you say, you would also have been down the street in two seconds flat. So where is Maria now?'

Jaime brooded into his empty glass. 'I'm dropping her back at the airport in Perth tomorrow. She's staying with Mum. And I, on the other hand, am sleeping here at the hotel, just in case she shows up in my bedroom,' he said to Mark.

Harold grumbled, 'You should be sleeping in jail.'

Jaime pulled a face at him. 'Even that would be preferable. She couldn't get to me there. Give me a break, Harold. I had no idea Maria wouldn't take no for an answer. And now I've lost my last chance with Peta. I threw it away.'

'Go after her, Jaime. If she really means that much to you,' Harold said. 'But be warned, I will be there to make sure that you make the trip to the altar with her this time, or you'll have to answer to me.'

Jaime shook his head. 'It's too late, Harold, she won't take me back a third time.'

Mark intervened. 'Don't be too sure,' he said. 'Go

and see her when you take Maria to the airport. At least give her an explanation. She deserves it.'

'What if she won't listen?'

'Then you'll get no less than you deserve.'

Mark knew his sister too well.

Chapter Nineteen

It took ages for Jaime to convince Maria he'd never marry her and just as long to console his mother, to make her understand that his heart belonged to the woman he'd lost twice. The one the tattoo over his heart symbolised forever. But Maria wasn't a woman who would take no for an answer.

The final scene at his mother's house had not been a pretty one, especially when Jaime explained the extent of the trouble Maria had caused. His mother had been in a state of shock when she discovered the existence of a grandchild, which had then turned to frantic sobbing when she realised that she may never get to meet the little girl. Peta may not be her choice of an ideal wife for her son, but a grandchild was a different matter altogether. Maria had been sullen, like a spoilt child whose favourite toy had been taken away.

'Now once and for all, Maria, I have no interest in marrying you. Ever. I don't love you. Hell, I don't even like you very much. Go home and find yourself the rich man you seem so determined to capture. I am a grown man, and I will choose my own wife. Although now, thanks to the two of you, I have probably lost the only woman who ever meant anything to me at all.' He'd stormed out after that and gone down to the bar where Harold had found him and nearly ripped his head off.

The longer he waited, the more agitated Jaime became knowing every moment he was away from Peta counted. Every delay gave her the opportunity to fly away again. He pressed his hand to the tattoo on his chest and tried to still the stabbing pain that thought brought with it as he escorted Maria into the airport, waited as she passed through security and the point of no return, making sure she understood it was over. He did not want her getting off the plane again the moment his back was turned.

Satisfied she'd gone; he made his way through the crowd towards the airport doors and sped down the freeway to Peta's penthouse, ignoring the beauty of the Swan River and the modern architecture that had consumed the city skyline over the years. Glancing at the address Mark had given him, he pulled up in the parking lot. Taking the entrance stairs two at a time, cursing the pain and stiffness in his leg, he found the elevator bank. Breathing deeply, he punched the button for the penthouse.

'Oh, you won't find anyone at home, love.'

He turned to look at the woman in her bright yellow tracksuit with a ratbag of a dog tucked under her arm.

She smiled sympathetically at him.

'Peta and Bella left yesterday.'

Jaime groaned, his heart sinking to his shoes. He was too late. He pushed down the panic that gripped his stomach. What to do now? He couldn't let her fly away again. Thanking the neighbour, he ran back to his car and drove to the second address on his list — Peta's mother's house. Jaime hammered at the door until he heard footsteps coming down the hallway.

'Jaime?' Mary Johnson pulled open the door, her face pale, eyes wide. 'What do you want?'

Oh, good God, he hadn't meant to scare her, but if she'd meddled in their lives again, he'd never forgive her. He tried to ease the scowl from his face and curb the impatience that chafed at his good sense. 'Where is she, Mary?'

'Who?'

Jaime blew out a long breath. Who else would he be looking for? 'I need to find her. Please tell me where she is.'

Mary huffed and placed her hands on her hips. 'You've come to the wrong door if you think I'm going to help you. Don't you think you've done enough damage?'

Jaime shook his head. 'I don't think we want to get into a discussion on who has done Peta the most damage, Mary. I would say that you are just as guilty of that as I am. Peta knows you and my parents connived to keep us apart. That you destroyed my letters and intercepted my phone calls when I tried to contact her. Now I'm running out of time and patience. Where is she?'

Mary's lips thinned. 'Peta chose not to confide in me about what happened in Williams. All I know is that she came back and packed her bags, leaving me to sort out her mess as usual. As if I have time for all this. If she wanted you to know, she would have told you herself where she was off to.'

She tried to push the door closed but Jaime blocked it. 'Please, Mary. Help me out here.'

Mary's lips remained stubbornly shut.

He tried again. 'You know, there was a time when you actually liked me. How come your opinion can change so quickly when things don't go the way you want them to? I loved your daughter then and I love her even more now. I thought I was doing the right thing by leaving and giving her space to grow up. I might even have come back for her, but between you and my family, you made that impossible. Instead, you rushed her into the arms of a violent man with a serious gambling problem and some pretty shady friends. If you want to hate me for what happened all those years ago, then go ahead, but please don't spoil my last chance to make things right.'

Mary had the grace to look ashamed. She'd know he was right, that forcing Peta and Paul together had been a mistake.

'He might have been good to her and Bella at first, but he went off the rails when he opened that damn nightclub and ended up in the wrong company. She won't be in that kind of danger with me, Mary. I can promise you that.' He waited, watching her chew her lip as she processed what he'd said.

She stepped aside with a sigh. 'Come inside, Jaime. She flew to Sydney. From there she's flying to Auckland to stay with her uncle for a while. I'll give you her itinerary. But be warned, if you mess with her again, you had better run fast and very far because this time I will deal with you myself.'

Jaime grinned, dizzy with relief. 'Join the queue, Mary,' he said. 'I have had that same warning issued so many times in the last twenty-four hours that I'm just not scared anymore.'

Mary gave a glimmer of a smile as she retrieved Peta's itinerary from the fridge door and handed it to him.

Jaime took the printout from her hands and bent to kiss her cheek. 'I promise I will not hurt her again. If she sends me packing, I'll go and never come back again.' The pain of that thought was almost too much to bear. 'But if she decides to give me another chance, not you, my parents or anyone else will ever come between us again.'

Mary read the underlying warning in his voice and nodded. 'I'm sorry, Jaime, for all the trouble we've caused the two of you. I only did what I thought was best for my daughter at the time. Good luck. Now get moving. Your time is running out.' She pointed to the paper he was crushing in his hands. Gently she pushed him out the door and waved him away down the drive.

Jaime wasted no time getting back to the airport. According to her itinerary, Peta's plane left for Auckland the following morning. If he could get a seat on the next plane to Sydney, he may be able to catch her at the international airport.

He made his way to the standby desk where seconds later the flight attendant shook her head regretfully. 'I'm sorry, you've just missed the last flight.'

Jaime swore silently. 'When is the next one?'

She consulted her list. 'Tomorrow morning at five.'

Jaime rubbed a weary hand over his face. He'd be cutting it fine.. 'Can you get me on it?'

The flight attendant consulted the list again. 'The only seat I have left is in First Class,' she replied.

'I'll take it.' Jaime handed over his credit card. She processed it and handed him his ticket. He wandered through to the passenger lounge and flopped into a chair to wait, praying he would make it in time.

He heard a voice calling his name through the thick fog of sleep. Jaime sat up, rubbing his eyes. An attractive flight attendant stood over him. A few months ago, he might have flirted with her, now he just wanted her to get him to Sydney fast. 'Your flight is about to be called, Mr Caruso,' she said.

'Thanks.' He stretched his cramped muscles and made his way to the gate.

The flight still seemed endless no matter how good First Class was and even if he felt like drinking, no amount of alcohol could dull his pain or impatience. He paced the floor, soothing the muscle in his leg, flicked through the movie channels and tried to listen to music. None of it could stop him thinking about losing Peta.

Four hours and ten anxious minutes later, they arrived in a wet and stormy Sydney. Jaime's heart fixed in his throat. What if they couldn't land? What if the plane got diverted because of the weather? What if he was too late?

He would follow her without question, but Auckland was a big town and she'd be hard to find. Although, she probably wouldn't consider that he'd come after her. He hadn't the first time. Finding her once she got there would take precious time. Always considering she wanted to be found, of course. Panic rose in his throat. He had to find her.

Relief flooded him as the captain announced that they would be able to land safely. He glanced at his watch. He had a little under an hour to get off the plane, through the airport from domestic to international. Not nearly enough time. He cursed the pain in his leg that slowed him down. Hopefully Peta and Bella hadn't progressed through Customs yet. If they had … no, he couldn't afford to think he'd lose them this time.

Jaime had a hard time keeping his feet still as he waited for the plane to taxi to a stop and the seatbelt light to go out. He shot out the door as soon as the flight attendant opened it. He played dodge as he ran through the crowded airport, praying his leg would hold up. As he neared the international side he heard the announcement.

'This is a call for all passengers on Flight 332 to Auckland to please proceed through Customs immediately. Thank you.'

'Please don't let it be too late,' he prayed as he shouldered his way through to where a queue of people lined up at the security check point. It was Bella he saw first.

'Bella!'

Peta heard the shout and felt the tug on her sleeve as Bella swung around.

'Daddy!' she called. 'Mum, my dad's here.' She bounced up and down, her excitement tearing at Peta's heart.

Peta looked over to where Jaime made his way towards them. No, she couldn't go through this again. She didn't want to hear excuses or explanations that would give her hope of happy-ever-afters. 'Come on, love, the man is waiting to check our hand luggage. We must go.' She placed an arm around Bella's shoulder and tried to guide her through.

Bella pulled free of Peta's restraining arm. 'No. I want to see my dad.' She ran to meet Jaime and threw herself into his arms.

Peta sighed and reluctantly vacated her place in the queue. What was it about Jaime that had girls of all ages throwing themselves at him? She made her way towards them.

Jaime hugged Bella tightly. He stood up as Peta approached, holding onto Bella's hand.

Peta stopped in front of him. 'We have to go, Jaime. It's too late.'

'Not until you let me explain,' he answered.

She shook her head. 'There's nothing to explain. You have a fiancée. You're committed. We're going to miss our flight.' Peta glanced down and saw Bella's grip on Jaime's hand tighten, her little fingers white with the effort. 'Bella, please, you have to let Jaime go and come with me now.'

'Please,' he begged. 'I need to talk to you. Please don't get on that plane. I can't lose you again. Please give me another chance.'

Peta sighed. She glanced around, embarrassed to see they had attracted an audience. And damn it, Jaime decided to use it as an advantage. Letting go of Bella's hand, he went down on one knee and took Peta's hand instead.

'Wait, what are you doing? Oh no, Jaime …'

'Peta, I made a big mistake letting you go, then and now. I am lost without you. I have missed you so much. I never want to see you walk away again. I wish I could change the past, but I can't, so I'd rather change the future with you. Will you please give me a chance to explain?' He turned her hand palm up and placed a kiss there, curling her fingers around it. 'I love you. I love my daughter. I'd like us to spend the rest of our lives together, as a family.'

It sounded like heaven after the hell they'd been through, but it wouldn't change a thing. It wouldn't make a difference to what his family wanted for him. Her mum might finally be seeing the consequences of her actions, and Peta could forgive her for her part in separating them all those years ago, but his mum still clung to her dream for him. It had been there in the clutch of her hands and the happiness on her face at seeing him and Maria together. A look that had haunted Peta's thoughts since walking away. This time he'd come after her. Could it be enough? Did it mean he really cared or was it only for Bella's sake?

She'd been running for so long. If she at least gave him his chance to explain, she could walk away knowing they'd cleared the air between them. If she lost this last chance of happiness with the man she loved, it would be with a clear conscience. He promised forever, but what if that was just another lie? What if it was the truth?

Pushing the doubts aside, she pulled her hand from his. 'Get up, you idiot. The whole airport is watching.'

He stood, hands at his sides, his gaze pleading, his smile gone.

'We need to go somewhere a little less public for this discussion.' She looked back at him, trying desperately to keep the hope out of her eyes.

Releasing a breath on a long sigh of relief, he drew her into his arms, closed them tightly around her and buried his face against her hair, his heart beating rapidly. 'Thank you, baby.'

'You don't get to call me that yet.'

Gently, he raised her chin with his forefinger and stared into her eyes. 'Do I get to kiss you?'

Peta shrugged, a smile teasing the corners of her mouth. She'd be mad to say no. 'Okay. Maybe just this once.'

'I plan to do it a whole lot more than once.'

He lowered his lips to hers and her resolve melted amidst the heat and taste of Jaime, whose mouth promised sweet things to come. He withdrew from her slowly as their audience around them broke into applause. 'Let's get out of here,' he said to Peta, slipping one hand in hers and the other taking Bella's.

'Our luggage …'

'I'll arrange for it to be retrieved and held for a flight change,' he reassured her.

She watched the girls on the flight desk fall for his charm and nudge each other when he smiled, but his fingers were threaded with hers and his eyes were only on her. Peta caught the look of envy on the flight attendants' faces and smiled as he secured their seats on a return flight to Perth.

Too exhausted to resist, Peta let her head rest against Jaime's shoulder. She couldn't summon up the energy to remove her hand, so she left her fingers entwined with his against his thigh and closed her eyes. The buzz of inflight noise floated through her sub — conscious as she dozed, Jaime's warmth solid and reassuring in the seat in between her and Bella.

She opened her eyes as the plane bumped down on the tarmac in Perth and taxied along the runway, and heard Jaime say, 'Bella, sweetheart, would you mind very much if we dropped you at Uncle Mark's house for a while when we get home?'

Bella looked at him, her eyes sad. 'Are you going to leave us again?'

Jaime shook his head. 'I'm not going anywhere, sweetheart, but your mum and I have a lot we need to talk about first, okay?' Bella nodded and Jaime hugged her tightly. 'Whatever happens, I will always be there if you need me.'

Three hours later they dropped a sleepy Bella at Mark's door. Mark wore a very smug look on his face as he and Bella waved them down the driveway. They drove in silence, each wrapped up in their own thoughts and doubts until Peta asked, 'Where are we going?'

'Somewhere where we can't be disturbed,' he replied.

Minutes later he pulled the car into a secluded area down by the river. Memories rushed back. Memories of those long sultry summer nights on a blanket under the trees, youth and discovering the joys of love.

He walked around to her side of the car and opened the door, holding out his hand. 'Remember?'

She placed her hand in his, her palm cool against his warm one. 'Yes.'

Oh God, yes. She remembered every tender moment they'd had there, every sweet, innocent touch and kiss until they'd taken it beyond that to a level she hadn't understood then but wanted now.

They walked down to the riverbank, their hands swinging between them, where the water lapped at their feet until they reached the tiny alcove secluded by the trees. Jaime sat and tugged Peta down until she sat in the V of his outstretched legs and her back rested against his chest. He folded his arms around her, and they watched the last rays of the setting summer sun sparkle on the water.

Jaime sighed. 'I owe you an explanation about Maria.'

'I guess you do.'

With his heart beating rapidly against her back, Peta relaxed against him, absorbing his strength. All she wanted was to put all this behind them and start over, whatever their future together held. She was tired, so very tired of running, fighting, and the disappointment that came with the struggles.

He picked up a handful of river sand and let it slide through his fingers. Peta imagined those long fingers sliding down her body, working their magic on her senses and turning her to jelly in his hands. She gave her thoughts a little shake and concentrated on Jaime's words as they fell into the silence between them.

'I am not and never will be engaged to Maria. Our families thought it might be a great merger. Two old families from the valley coming together sounded like a great idea. But it's not what I want.'

'It looked like she wanted it and your mum looked

pretty happy about that.' Still the old insecurities niggled at her mind, eating away at hope.

'She's gone for good, Peta. I put her on a plane and made sure she left right before I came looking for you. There will be no further misunderstandings or interference. Not from Maria, not from my parents and definitely not from your mother. I give you my absolute word that I'm here for the long haul,' he promised.

'I believe you, Jaime,' she reassured him, seeing his searching look. Peta smiled sadly as she heard him exhale in relief. 'But there'll always be that part of me waiting for you to change your mind again.'

She stood up and wandered back down to the river's edge. Her pulse raced as Jaime came up behind her to stand close. His heat against her back sent delicious shivers down her spine. She wanted to turn around and bury herself in his warmth, let him kiss away the doubt that churned inside her. Instead, she fought to focus on settling the questions between them. It had to be done before they could move forward. She folded her arms under her breasts but couldn't resist leaning back against him.

He moved closer and placed his arms around hers, his chin against her hair. She wanted to settle in his arms, forget what had happened in the past and make new memories instead, but if they didn't lay the ghosts and doubt to rest, they'd always be a barrier between them.

'What if we've changed too much, Jaime?' The words came out husky and emotional, more so than she'd intended them to be.

'Then we'll work through it together,' he reassured her.

'What if we go through all this again only to discover that marriage still scares you and you find the permanency stifling? Will you run away again, Jaime?' Peta tipped her head back against his shoulder and looked up at him.

Jaime kissed her forehead. 'No, this time there's no running away. I made that mistake once. I do try to learn from my mistakes. I have spent ten long years comparing other women to you, Peta. None of them ever measured up.'

'Why didn't you call me, or write to me, or bloody hell, even send me a text? You stayed in touch with Mark.'

Jaime shrugged and held her closer. 'I often thought of contacting you, but I was under the impression that you were happily married and didn't want to make any waves. There didn't seem any point to rubbing salt into my wounds.' He sighed. 'Mark used to talk about you every time we caught up over the years, but he never let on that your marriage wasn't a happy one.'

'I swore him to secrecy, especially when things started going wrong. Then Paul got in deeper with Albero and Bennetti. I didn't want Mum to know that we had an outlaw gang frequenting the club or that Paul was into anything other than running The Golden Diva. I had to protect my family. Beyond Hell's Reach don't like snitches. In the end, I couldn't. Paul got Bella anyway.'

'And now you have her back.'

'Yes, I have her back and Paul is locked away. The focus is off me, and The Golden Diva will be shut down for good with the evidence Mark has.' She sighed, the reality of that door closing in her life sinking in. 'It's over.'

Jaime turned her around in his arms, their bodies touching, igniting fires that cried out for satiation. She moved closer, seeking the comfort of his warmth. Peta reached up and touched his face, needing to feel his skin against her palm, to make sure he was really there with his arms around her and not just another dream that would fade with the sunrise.

He turned his head and placed a kiss in her palm. 'Where do we go from here?'

Peta shook her head. 'I really don't know, Jaime. I want to believe that this is happening, but I can't help wondering if it's too good to be true. It's not just ourselves we have to consider. Bella might get hurt if you decide fatherhood isn't for you and I couldn't bear for that to happen.'

Jaime pressed her head down against his shoulder and kissed the top of her head. 'How about we give it a trial? That's what we'd agreed to before this fiasco. Remember, one step at a time?' He stroked her hair, a soothing movement that had her relaxing against him. 'We won't make any permanent plans until we're both comfortable with our progress. It will give me a chance to get to know Bella and for her to get used to me.'

'Are you angry with me for not telling you about her?' Peta asked.

Jaime shook his head. 'No, I understand your reasons for not telling me. I am sorry I missed so much of her life, but I will make it up to both of you. Let's leave the past where it belongs and work together on building our future. We have a lot of good years left. Let's use them to our advantage.'

'One day at a time?' Peta searched his face for any traces of doubt and found none.

'One day at a time,' he agreed.

His face was close to hers, their lips a millisecond apart. Peta met him halfway, winding her arms around his neck to pull him closer. She felt the heat of his arousal against her stomach and snuggled closer. He sighed as he nibbled at her lower lip.

'God, I've missed your taste.'

His arms tightened as she recaptured his mouth with crushing intensity. Her hands strayed under his shirt, running them along the hard muscular contours. Jaime's lips made slow progress down her neck, nipping at the pulse at the base of her throat, turning her knees weak until she collapsed against him. He placed a hand on her buttocks and lifted her against his rigidness so she could feel his need. Peta closed her eyes and sighed as his hand found her breast and gently caressed the peaks.

'Jaime,' she whispered, opening her eyes to meet his gaze full of hot need in the fading light.

His cheeks dimpled in a smile as he moved his mouth and whispered something against her ear, but she heard nothing, the roar of blood in her head drowning out his words, the smell of his cologne filling her senses and the taste of his skin only a whisper away.

His breath against her ear sent her imagination into overdrive. She closed her eyes and absorbed the sensation, trying to remember how to breathe. The grip on her bottom tightened, forcing her to look at him again. He closed the gap between their mouths and the world around her faded away, leaving only Jaime.

Her lips parted on a whisper, inviting him in. His tongue explored her mouth, seeking, deepening when she matched him stroke for stroke. His palm rested on her thigh at the hemline of her skirt, fingers playing on the sensitive skin, inching the material up. Peta reached for his face and brought him closer still, the feel of him in her hands turning the sweet ache inside her to a burn.

Jaime's arms tightened around her, drawing her up against him to feel the heat that pulsed between them. Warmth flooded her and she arched her hips against his, desperate to feel him where she needed him to be. His hands ran a path down her spine, fire trailing in their wake then his hand cupped her bottom, pressed her closer and she found the comfort of his length, rode it, wanted it to end this desperate need for him.

Peta gave her hands free reign and flicked loose the buttons on his shirt. She slid her hand inside and ran her palm across his chest, thrilling in the feel of the coarse hair against her skin. She felt him hesitate before breaking contact with her lips. He pressed her hand closer with his.

For a second their eyes met, his full of promise, before he kissed the sensitive spot below her earlobe and trailed down to her neck, nibbling at her skin.

Her blouse drifted off her shoulder and he kissed the exposed skin. Peta arched her neck, swallowing a whimper as he continued a path down towards her breasts where she welcomed his lips. Pulling his shirt from his jeans, her hands roamed the contours of his back, up into his hair, holding his head against her heart.

Jaime's lips moved to her beautiful firm breasts, nipped at the pebbled nipples. Ripples of ecstasy flowed over her skin as she reached for his belt, loosening it with desperate fingers. Then she lowered his zipper to encase his length in her hand—warm, silky and ready as he pressed into her palm.

Lifting his head, he laid his forehead against hers, his breath coming in short bursts. Jaime pulled her blouse together. She wanted to stop his hands from doing up the buttons, drag them back to her body, but they fisted on the edges of the material that covered her breasts.

'Sweet Jesus, Peta. Any more of that and I won't be able to stop,' he whispered against her head.

'Then don't.' She'd resort to begging if she had to. Tonight was for rediscovery, tomorrow their journey would begin again. Now was for them and the fire that burned inside them, ready to cleanse the ghosts of the past.

She'd make him stop thinking. Tonight had no place for second thoughts, not if they wanted to move forward. She dropped butterfly light kisses along his jaw, her tongue finding the cleft in his chin.

His hands moved over her shoulders and eased her blouse down, the cool evening air sending a trail of goosebumps across her skin. Jaime kissed her lips before following the trail of his hands. He found the zipper and eased her skirt down over her hips, watching her face for signs of hesitation or doubt. He wouldn't find any. Not tonight, not ever. Then she stood before him naked, and he stepped back.

'God, you're beautiful, Peta.' His voice filled with pride. 'I've missed you so much. I want to go to sleep holding you, wake up with you next to me. Promise me you'll stay.'

Peta smiled at him. Hesitating only slightly, she moved forward to remove his shirt while he stepped out of his jeans. 'I'm not going anywhere,' she whispered.

They stood close, their bodies touching, the heat between them enough to ward off the cool night air.

'No doubts?' he whispered, nibbling at her ear. 'All you have to do is say the word and I'll stop.'

Peta shook her head and dropped fiery kisses across his chest. She buried her nose in the light sprinkling of hair across his chest and inhaled his scent.

He lowered her onto the soft grass. Their lips met and clung. Tasting, releasing and sipping again, like a wine that needed to be savoured, appreciated. Jaime broke the kiss and looked into her eyes as his hands worked their magic on her body. Murmuring soft words, his hands moved down her body, gliding, moulding and loving, starting little fires under her skin.

His hands found the spot where she ached for him most, stroking and teasing until she was wet against his fingers, writhing under him, begging him to come to her. Jaime lowered himself until they were matched hip-to-hip, thigh-to-thigh. His hard, satiny length pressed against her. Peta drew his head down, her lips clinging to his while her body arched against his. He rose on his arms, and she parted her thighs for him, ready to cradle him there. Slowly he descended and guided his length inside her, his eyes on hers.

Together they began the gentle rhythm as old as time

and Peta's body accepted him willingly, stretched to accommodate him fully. Heat and passion built to frenzy as they moved together, whispering between kisses. Then the world exploded around them, and Jaime cried out as his warmth flooded her. She clung to his shoulders, his faced pressed into her neck where his breathing feathered her skin and held on for the journey back to reality.

Jaime lifted his head and kissed her forehead, her nose, her cheeks then he rolled onto his back, taking her with him so that she lay cradled on his chest, her head on his thundering heart. One hand on the small of her back held her to him, the other drew circles up and down her back. 'I thought we were going to take this one step at a time?'

'That was a step, wasn't it?' she teased.

'We have to be sensible, Peta. I don't want to rush things. We have to get it right this time.' He caressed her face gently.

That was at least one thing they agreed on, Peta thought silently. As beautiful as this time between them was, they still had fences to mend. 'It's time for another step, Jaime. We need to get this thing sorted with your parents.'

'I know, but I'd like to spend more time with you and Bella before we do.' He kissed her hard before gently lifting her off him and rolling her aside. 'Let's go pick up our daughter.'

She slipped her hand into his and let him pull her up. 'Let's do that.'

In the car, he turned and said, 'This time, we're getting married. I won't leave you behind again.'

Peta smiled. 'I'm ready. Are you?'

He looked down at her and grinned. 'You're stuck with me now. I won't make the same mistake again.' He leaned over and kissed her hard.

'I think I can handle having you around.' She placed a hand on his thigh and squeezed.

He held it there for a moment before straightening up and starting the car. 'Good, because I'm never letting you go. We're in this together for the long haul, baby.'

'And if Maria comes back?'

He shuddered. 'It'll be your turn to send her packing.'

'I can do that.' Peta smiled as he put the car in gear and pulled away. 'I think I might even enjoy it.'

Jaime chuckled. 'I love you, Peta.'

'Don't ever stop saying it.'

The short drive to Mark's house was filled with fleeting touches, warm smiles, and promises of more when night had settled in, Bella was asleep, and they were alone again. Mark grinned from ear to ear when he opened the door to them.

'Hey, you two, did you get everything sorted out?' he asked, sighing with relief when they nodded and smiled at each other. 'Come on in then. Bella's like a bloody cat on hot bricks. She's been bouncing between the window and the television since you left.' His grin said he had no problem with that at all.

'She'll keep you on your toes, Markie boy.' Peta pressed a finger against his stomach. 'Keeps you in shape.'

Jaime held out his arms as Bella rushed towards them. 'Hello, sweetheart,' he said, hugging her tightly like he was still having a hard time believing it. 'Ready to go home?'

Bella smiled brightly and nodded. 'Yeah!'

Peta watched the two together, a warm feeling encompassing her heart and with a flash of insight, knew it would all work out. How could it not? Mark put his arm around her. Peta looked up at him and hugged him around his waist.

'Thank you. For everything,' she said.

'You're welcome. I hope the two of you will be very happy together. You deserve to be.' He hugged her back.

'Your turn will come,' she told him.

He laughed. 'I'm not finished playing playboy yet. Cut me some slack here.'

Peta grinned. 'Your days are numbered, my boy. Once word gets around that you're no longer my personal escort and bodyguard, you've had it. Half the town will be queuing up at your door. You're far too much of a hero to be alone. Just remember whoever you pick has to pass my test first.'

'Well, that should scare them all away then. Lucky I'm moving to Perth. Harold and I have been assigned to head up the taskforce investigation into the connection between the Perth chapter of Beyond Hell's Reach and the Tag Raiders. We need to get ice off the streets. Bennetti and Albero have moved operations from Melbourne to Perth now that The Golden Diva is closed, and they've lost their cover.'

Peta shivered. 'Be careful, Mark. Those guys are brutal. I don't like it, but I know what you have to do.'

'You're safe. That's what matters. Now I have to make the streets safe too.'

Jaime and Bella joined them. 'Looks like I'm your bodyguard now,' Jaime teased.

Mark removed his hands from Peta's shoulders and held them up in the air. 'She's all yours, mate. You have no idea how exhausting it is playing bodyguard to a superstar.' He dodged the punch Peta aimed at his arm.

'Just as well I know how to tame her then.'

'Oh God, I don't want to know.' Mark covered his ears with his hands.

Jaime grinned. 'Well, let's go, guys. We have to see if your room at the Williams Hotel is still available,' Jaime prompted.

Much later, fed and housed in the honeymoon cottage in the picturesque gardens behind the Williams Hotel, they settled Bella down for the night.

'You never did say how you managed to track me

down,' Peta reminded Jaime as they shared a mug of steaming coffee.

'I went to see your mother,' he replied with a grimace.

Peta's eyebrows flew up. 'That was a brave move. How was she?'

Jaime pulled a face. 'At first, I thought she would beat me to a pulp with her broomstick. But once I explained it all to her, she was okay.'

Peta laughed. 'You're lucky. A few years ago, she was ready to hang you.'

Jaime shivered. 'Scary thought, I hate that we wasted all this precious time.'

Peta hugged him. 'But think of all the fun we're going to have making up for lost time.'

He kissed her hard. She returned it, tasting the eagerness on his lips.

'Stay here tonight,' she whispered.

A moment of panic seized her. She didn't want him out of her sight. But Jaime was not going to run again, she tried to reassure herself. He was just being sensible, and she needed to be too. They needed to pace themselves so that emotion didn't rule over sensibility.

He read the panic in her eyes and pressed kisses over them. 'Peta, there's nothing I would like more than to take you into that bedroom and show you again just how much I love you and have missed you, but that would defeat the purpose. We have to take things one step at a time. I promised you that and by God, you're going to get it. And at the end of it all, there will be no doubts left that we belong together, forever.'

Peta bit her lip and nodded. He ran a finger over her lips before placing a kiss on them. She knew he was right. Neither of them needed to rush into anything, they had the rest of their lives.

Chapter Twenty

Peta tucked the covers around Bella and kissed her forehead. In the two weeks since they'd returned to Perth, life with Jaime was everything she'd dreamed about. The bond between him and his daughter grew stronger every day. Sometimes the resemblance between them, the connection they had, took her breath away.

'Good night, sweetheart.'

'Night.' Bella snuggled down and pulled the covers up to her chin. 'Mum?'

'Yes?' Peta smiled and smoothed her daughter's hair back from her face. Sleepy like this, she could see so much of Jaime in her features.

'When can I meet my nonna and nonno?'

'Soon, I promise.'

The last hurdle they still had to conquer. Seeing

Jaime's parents again. Reliving the events of the past and dealing with the fallout of the last time they'd tried. Hopefully this time there'd be no unpleasant surprises.

'Will you ask my dad when?'

'I will, sweetheart. But remember Dad is very busy at work at the moment.'

The company's transition from Williams to Perth had begun. As his new job demanded his attention, Peta watched and waited on edge in case Jaime became bored with them. Waiting for that moment when he'd decide this wasn't what he wanted.

Peta sighed. The longer they delayed it, the harder it would be to face the demons of their past. For Bella's sake, they couldn't put it off any longer. Time was limited as Jaime's dad's illness progressed. She owed it to him to let him spend what was left of that time with the grandchild he'd missed seeing grow up.

Surely their relationship was strong enough to cope with any obstacles now. Together they could overcome the doubt, prove that this time they were in it for the long haul and nothing or no one could come between them again.

'We'll see. You go to sleep now, okay?' Peta turned off the light next to her bed. No need for one anymore now that the memories of what had happened in Williams were fading, replaced by the happiness and balance of family she'd always wanted for her daughter. She just had to make it last a lifetime. 'Love you.'

'Love you too, Mum.'

Peta smiled and pulled the door closed, walking down the hallway to the lounge. Yes, the time had come to cross that last bridge, to take this to the next level. She wanted to wake up to Jaime's head on the pillow next to hers every morning and know they belonged together.

On the sofa, Jaime sat with his legs stretched out, feet crossed at the ankles, arms hugging his chest. His leg had healed well, the bullet now a memory etched into his skin in a red puckered scar that would fade over time. Like the bad memories that too would fade.

'Jaime, don't you think it's time?' Peta sat, curling her legs up under her and leaning against him.

He stretched his arms up then hugged her closer, pulling her snugly in the comfort of his hold. 'Time for what?'

'To settle things with your parents.'

Jaime looked at her, doubt clouding his eyes. 'It's too soon.'

'What are you scared of, Jaime? I don't think I'll be comfortable as long as the past hangs over our heads. It's time to take that next step, Jaime.' She ran a hand down his cheek, following the groove that became deeper as he clenched his jaw.

'Everything's going so well, Peta. I'm too scared to spoil it.'

His honesty touched her heart. 'I'm scared too, but

there's no point delaying it any longer. Now is a good time for it. Bella has settled well and the two of you are getting along so well. We need to get that last obstacle out of the way, the last one to stand between us.' Peta kissed the spot where his jaw knotted.

Jaime sighed. 'I know you're right, but ...'

'They won't scare me away. I'm a lot tougher than I was ten years ago. I think we're ready.' She filled her tone with confidence, even though her mind still harboured some doubt. Only after they'd confronted his parents could they truly move on.

'Okay,' he agreed finally. 'We'll go over there tomorrow morning. I have to see Dad about finalising their move to Perth and putting the house up for sale. But after that, will you marry me, make this official?'

Peta nibbled his ear. 'One step at a time,' she whispered.

'Then you'd better stop what you're doing, or we'll be taking a leap rather than a step,' he replied, but didn't pull away. Instead, he turned his head and caught her lips, kissing her very thoroughly. 'Now behave, or I won't be responsible for my actions.' He pulled her onto his lap and pushed them both to the limit, kissing a path down her neck, across her collarbone to where her cleavage rose above the neckline of her shirt.

She squirmed in his lap, her need for him too great to ignore, then she dragged his head up and kissed him until her head spun and his hands gripped her hips to hold her closer.

'I don't want to be responsible anymore,' he whispered against her lips. 'I'd like a baby brother or sister for Bella.'

'I'd like that too.' Peta kissed a trail across his cheek to his ear. 'Come to bed with me. Let's be irresponsible, just this once.'

'Once won't be enough.' He moaned as she nipped his earlobe. 'We have years of practice to catch up on.'

'Then stop wasting precious time.'

He cupped her face in his hands, drawing her gaze to his. 'Are you sure?'

Peta rested her forehead against his. 'Yes.'

And even though the butterflies somersaulted in her stomach as he lifted her up and carried her to her bedroom, kicking the door closed behind them, she knew exactly what she wanted. Jaime's brand of love, forever.

As they made the trip from Perth to Williams to his parent's house, Peta smiled despite her nervousness. It was hard to believe that her life had seemed to begin and end in this small town a lifetime ago. Now they'd arrived at another new beginning again. She prayed with all her heart that this time it would be all right. They pulled up in the driveway with a sense of *déjà vu*.

Peta eyed Jaime, her eyebrow arched, her gaze wary. 'Want to check for surprise fiancées before we go in?' She grinned.

'Very funny.' Jaime grimaced. 'The only one likely to launch herself at me today is my mother, armed with a frying pan because I've stayed away this long,' he joked, but leaned over and hugged her fiercely. 'Let's do this.'

Taking a deep breath and letting it out on a sigh, Jaime led them to the front door. 'Right, here goes …' He turned the handle and pushed the door open. Turning back to Peta and Bella, he took their hands. Smiling reassuringly, he urged them along the hallway as he called, 'Mum, Dad?'

His mother bustled out of the kitchen, wiping flour off her hands with a kitchen towel. She burst into a spate of Italian and hugged him, leaving a huge flour imprint on his back. Bella looked at Peta and giggled, pointing to the mark as Jaime wriggled out of his mother's embrace. He kissed her cheeks and stepped aside to pull Peta and Bella forward.

'Mum, I think it's time you met the woman I want to marry. You remember Peta?'

Peta bent forward a little to receive a kiss on both cheeks then returned it. 'Hello, Mrs Caruso. You're looking well. It's been a long time.'

'Thank you, yes.' She offered a hesitant smile. 'And welcome.'

Jaime patted his mother's shoulder. 'Mum, this is your granddaughter, Bella, who assures me she speaks fluent Italian.' He drew Bella to stand between them, his hands on her shoulders. 'Say hi to Nonna, sweetheart.'

'Buona sera, Nonna. Come stai?'

Bella stood on tiptoe to kiss her grandmother's flushed cheeks. Mrs Caruso stood silently for a second, wringing her hands in the kitchen towel, obviously trying to decide what to do next.

'Well …' She folded the cloth into a neat square and shoved it into the pocket of her apron. 'Welcome to the family. Now, Jaime, find your father and take Bella to meet him. He's having a good day today. Peta and I have a few things to discuss.' She turned away towards the kitchen. 'Come along, Peta.'

Peta looked at Jaime hesitantly. He kissed her hard. 'She'll behave,' he promised. 'She knows I mean business.' To Bella he said, 'Let's go and find your nonno.'

Peta watched them go before heading through to the kitchen, her heart in her throat. This had to work. It had to go well. 'Hmm, smells good,' she commented as she sniffed at the delicious aromas of fresh homemade bread mixed with baking pasta. 'That has to be the famous Caruso lasagne.'

Mrs Caruso looked at her in surprise. 'How do you know?'

Peta smiled. 'Jaime brought a dish over to Mark's one day and shared it around. A long time ago.'

'And you remember this?' Mrs Caruso laughed. 'I didn't know it was that good. I'm surprised he shared it. Normally he would eat a whole dish by himself.'

It was Peta's turn to smile. 'He didn't have a choice that day. Mark practically tackled it out of his hands. Even I had to fight for a share.'

The tension in the room evaporated as they discussed a few favourite recipes until Mrs Caruso placed a cup of tea on the wooden kitchen table in front of Peta. 'Let's sit,' she said. 'We have a lot to talk about.'

A small shiver of apprehension tickled Peta's spine. Was this where she got warned off? Were they heading back down the same old path of rejection?

'Peta,' she began, 'I can't pretend that this is the marriage I wanted for my son.' She covered Peta's cold hands with her warm ones. 'That's not to say I disapprove. I was a stubborn, misinformed old woman who only wanted what was best for her son. This is something you will only understand when your daughter is making the same choices. I wanted for him what my parents wanted for me — a good, steady marriage, an arranged marriage. That is how I was married. Look how it turned out. Good. I learned to love the man my parents chose for me, but then maybe I was just lucky. He is a good man, like Jaime.'

She stood and collected some cookies from the jar and put them on a plate in front of Peta before continuing. 'Eat, you're too skinny. I am sorry for making trouble between you. We thought it was the right thing to do. We wanted him to take over the business when his dad retired. We didn't think about what he wanted. So, he left. If we'd lost him in Afghanistan …' She sighed. 'He tried to contact you, but I told your mother not to pass on any correspondence. We thought it would be best. But it wasn't.'

Peta nibbled on a cookie, giving an appreciative moan as chocolate melted on her tongue. She could almost forgive her future mother-in-law. Almost.

Mrs Caruso sighed heavily. 'When he came back here for the bush dance, he was different, unsettled but happier. Then Maria showed up and said they were engaged, I thought this must be the reason and that it had all worked out after all. But then we found out it was all a lie.' She shook her head. 'Jaime was very angry with Maria. I am sorry, Peta. We were blind not to have trusted our son's own judgement. Please forgive us for the heartache we have caused.'

Peta's eyes filled with tears as the woman wrung her hands anxiously. 'Mrs Caruso, people make mistakes. Perhaps it was a good thing you did interfere. I was very young then and very confused about where I was going in life. For Jaime to have married me because I was pregnant would have been a big mistake. Now we know for sure what we want. We want to be together, to be a family.' They smiled at each other as Peta placed her hands in the older woman's. 'I loved Jaime then, but it was puppy love. Now I love him for the man he has become. We can appreciate each other more now.'

Mrs Caruso beamed. 'Then welcome to the family. No more Mrs Caruso. It will be confusing enough with two of us.' She stood up and poured them each a sherry. Handing a glass to Peta, she said, 'To new beginnings and new families.'

They raised their glasses and drank the toast.

'But now, Jaime tells me you had some trouble of your own. I would very much like you to tell me about it so that I can understand.'

She listened patiently as Peta told her about their ordeal with Paul and how it had all come to an end. When the story was finished, she stood and hugged Peta tightly.

'You are a very brave girl,' she said. 'And now it's over. Now let's get these men fed before they help themselves.' Moving back to the stove, she waved Peta away. 'Go find your family and bring them in here.'

Peta hugged her before making her way to find Jaime. They met halfway down the corridor.

'Everything okay?'

She smiled and slipped her arms around him. 'All sorted.'

Jaime hugged and kissed her hard. 'Then we have a wedding to plan.'

Peta laughed as she wriggled out of his arms. 'Food first, I think. Your mother's gone to a lot of trouble to feed you.'

'Will you be dessert?' he asked hopefully.

'I think your mother's tiramisu will have to be demolished first, but if you eat all your food … you never know.' She pressed a kiss to his lips, took a moment to enjoy the taste knowing they'd be there any time she wanted them, forever. 'Now, get your father and daughter. The lasagne's getting cold.'

Reluctantly Jaime let her go. 'Lasagne, tiramisu, family and a beautiful woman—what more could a guy possibly need?'

'In that order?'

'Not necessarily.'

Chapter Twenty-One

The day of the wedding dawned, sunny and bright. Amidst the chaos of people rushing to fix last minute emergencies, Peta stood in her mother's guest bedroom wondering if her feet could get any colder.

Last minute doubts fought their way through her mind, but she squashed them stubbornly. No, this time there was no turning back. Whatever faced them in the future, they had to deal with it together. They'd made a deal.

She checked her appearance in the mirror, tucked away a few strands that had worked their way loose from the elegant hairstyle that made her look like Audrey Hepburn. The hairdresser had done a great job as had the makeup artist. She hardly recognised the face beneath the carefully arranged hair filled with miniature rosebuds the exact colour of her bouquet.

Mrs Caruso had done a magnificent job with her wedding dress. She smoothed her hand over the Italian lace inserts in the ivory satin dress that tapered at the waist and then flowed out around her in a swirl of softness.

'You look beautiful, Peta. You will take my son's breath away.' Mrs Caruso arranged her veil carefully. 'Be happy.'

Mindful of not crushing the beautiful flowers, Peta hugged her mother-in-law and then her mother. 'I will. You need never worry about that.'

Bella came into the room dressed in a replica of her mother's dress, hers the colour of pink antique roses. Her dark hair had been meticulously curled into ringlets and scooped back with ribbon to match her dress. Peta smiled at her daughter, who had blossomed with the attention she received from her new grandparents and father, the traumatic events that had brought them to this day now a distant memory.

'You look beautiful, princess,' Peta said, pride making her eyes sting with tears.

'So do you,' replied Bella. 'We're going to be so happy together, Mummy.'

Peta hugged her tightly. 'We sure are. Let's go make a family. Are you ready?' She took the little girl's hand.

Bella nodded eagerly curling her fingers around Peta's. 'I'm ready.'

At the church, Jaime waited nervously at the altar for his bride. What if she'd changed her mind? He cast a wary look at Harold where he sat in the front pew with Peta's parents, all muscle-bound and glowering expressions in his suit that looked like it made him itch. No, Harold definitely wasn't a suit man. He was more the jeans and polo shirt type. And the only thing soft about him was the smiling, curvy woman who sat next to him, her hand stilling the agitated bounce of his leg. Jeannie.

Jaime grinned at him. Harold's unspoken warnings were wasted today. He wasn't about to run out on this wedding, so Harold would have no reason to carry out his threat. His gaze turned back to Mark who fiddled nervously with the collar of his shirt and straightened his bowtie. His friend felt for the rings in his breast pocket for what must have been the hundredth time.

'You owe me big, mate,' he said, catching Jaime's amused grin. 'If I hadn't organised this reunion, you wouldn't be standing here today.'

'I think we have Paul Price to thank for that, the bastard. But you bet I owe you. Your meddling was my downfall. Not that I mind the fall.' He adjusted his own collar, which seemed to get a little tighter the faster the minutes ticked over. 'You'll get yours one day. Somewhere out there is the right woman for you.'

Mark frowned. 'Not me, mate. I'm too busy catching bad guys.'

'Speaking of bad guys …'

'You never need to worry about Price again. With the statement he's given us, we're hot on the heels of his dealers. It's only a matter of time until we catch them.' Mark patted his shoulder.

'As long as my girls are safe.'

'Safe as houses.'

The organist struck out the first strains of the *Bridal March* and the congregation stood.

'Here we go,' said Jaime and turned to watch his bride and their daughter make their way down the aisle towards a promising future. His heart filled with pride at the sight of his beautiful family, and he knew there was no place he'd rather be than here, waiting to take Peta's hand in his. The time for running was over. He had lost time to make up for and he planned to use every moment of the years ahead making them happy.

Peta reached him and he lifted her veil. He had no words for how she made him feel. Whole didn't seem to be a big enough word to describe it, but she made his heart pound and his knees weak. Without her he was nothing. He'd existed, not lived.

Her eyes met his and in them he saw love, promise, and tears he hoped were happiness. Then she smiled and he wanted to gather her in his arms and kiss her, forget about the audience watching and waiting for them to take their vows. But there'd be plenty of time for that.

He cupped her cheek with his palm. She leaned into his hand for a moment, closing her eyes, then he took her hand in his, Bella's in the other, and they turned to the priest to take their vows.

Mark finally closed the car door on the newlyweds and their daughter on Monday morning, sending them away on their honeymoon. He heaved a sigh of relief. 'Harold,' he said as he placed an arm around his partner's shoulders, 'that was a tough case. Thanks for your help.'

A grin lifted the corners of Harold's mouth. 'Jaime better treat those girls right. It's great to see her so happy.'

'Oh, I think he will,' Mark reassured him.

'Well, it's back to business then. Meet you at the office? I'll buy you a coffee because I'm as sure as shit not drinking that mud they have at the station.'

Mark's phone rang and he looked at the number, a frown furrowing his forehead as he answered, 'DSS Johnson.'

TJ Stevens, his favourite mechanic and go-to girl for rehabilitating drug-addicted kids, sounded breathless over the roar of an engine. 'Mark, you might want to follow me. I'm heading to the Tag Raiders clubhouse.'

'TJ, are you talking on a mobile phone while you're driving? Please tell me you're on handsfree so I don't have to issue you with a fine.'

'Yes, I'm talking on hands free. Here, ask my boss.'

A rustle over the line had Mark moving the phone away from his ear for a moment before a male voice answered, 'Scott Devin.'

'She wasn't on hands free, was she?' Mark chuckled.

'Uh … nope.'

'I didn't think so. Are you going with her to the clubhouse?'

'I guess?'

'Good. Last time she went down there, we brought her back in an ambulance. I don't want to have to do that again.'

'Of course not.'

'I'm Detective Senior Sergeant Mark Johnson. My partner Harold Jones and I will meet you down there. Try to keep her out of a brawl until we get there.' He hung up and turned to Harold. 'That celebratory coffee might have to wait. There's trouble at the Tag Raiders clubhouse and that can only mean Paul's buddies Albero and Bennetti must be hanging around.'

Harold was already halfway to the car. 'No rest for

the wicked.' He looked back over his shoulder. 'Who's driving?'

Mark pushed his phone into his pocket and pulled out his keys, tossing them in his palm. 'Me.'

'Fuck.'

Tagged (Unfinished Business,
Book 2)

Want to know what happens next? Join DSS Mark Johnson and his partner, Harold, as they tackle their next case.

Tagged (Unfinished Business, Book 2)

TJ Stevens will go to any lengths to protect the young offenders in her apprenticeship rehabilitation program. She's worked hard to keep them off the streets and out of trouble. With her new boss threatening to cancel the program and danger striking close to home for the youths, will Scott Devin be a trusted ally or yet another enemy?

When Scott Devin buys a struggling car dealership in semi-rural Western Australia, he knows he's buying a bucketload of trouble. He's just not expecting the mess he walks in on, or the reason for it. Heading up the challenge is a woman who fights like a tigress protecting her cubs against the dark underworld of crime. Can he afford to get involved in the danger she brings to his door?

Book 2 - Chapter 1

TJ pushed through the doors into the reception area of Mal's Motors, leaving them swinging behind her. 'Marty, I need a tow down on Albany Highway. Sheila's spat the dummy again,' she yelled. Her car was getting too old and unreliable to be out late. She'd pushed Sheila too hard last night, scouring the streets, looking for Tiny. She had no other choice, but a car that could break down at any time placed her in a vulnerable position in the dark alleyways where her boys found most of their trouble. Or rather, where trouble found them.

A man in a suit stepped in front of her. 'Are you TJ Stevens?'

'Yes. Sorry, I'll be with you in just a moment.'

TJ missed the disgruntled look he aimed her way as she set her hands on his forearms and steered him out of her path. She grabbed her uniform jacket off the peg and heaved open the connecting door to the workshop. There'd been no sign of Tiny, despite searching until almost dawn, and now she was over-tired from lack of sleep and later than late. 'Marty!'

'I got it, TJ,' the first-year apprentice yelled back.

'Take Tony with you. You know she won't let anyone else near her.'

'Got it.' Marty jogged toward her with a tow rope looped over his shoulder. 'There's someone to see you out front. Not happy that you're late.' He nodded toward the man she'd moved aside, who now paced the reception floor.

TJ tossed Marty her keys. 'I'll take care of it. Go and get Sheila before she gets a ticket. Tony! Let's get this done. We've got a big workload today.' She gave them directions to the broken-down car. 'Marty, have you seen Tiny lately?'

'Nah, TJ. I'm doing like you said and staying out of trouble.'

'Good lad. You'll let me know if he tries to contact you though, right?'

'Yeah, you know I will.'

'Cool. Go get my car now so we can start the day.'

With a sigh, she headed for the cloakroom and sat down on the bench to unstrap her stiletto sandals. The day hadn't even started yet, and already she had blisters. Not helped at all by the two-kilometre hike, thanks to

Sheila breaking down. She tugged on her uniform pants under her mini skirt.

Her mobile phone vibrated against the cold steel bench, the display showing an unknown caller. It skittered off the edge to fall face down in the greasy mop bucket. Luckily, the water had been drained.

'Looks like it's going to be one of those days.' Resigned to her fate, she fished her phone out of the grey sludge and wiped it on a rag.

'TJ? The bloke in reception says you need to get your butt out there now.' One of the technicians banged on the cloakroom door.

'I'll be out in a minute.' Work-worn, scarred safety boots replaced the heels, hastily tugged on over thick socks. The laces could wait. TJ strode back into the workshop, laces flapping against the concrete floor as she went.

'Back to work,' she called when she noticed that work had ground to a halt as her team watched her progress across the shop. TJ smiled at the comments, cat calls, grumbles and exaggerated sighs.

'Sheila ready for the scrap heap this time?'

'Blown a gasket has she?'

'Forget something, TJ?'

As leading hand, she was used to the teasing. The relationship she had with her team was a good one. They worked well together.

The connecting door back into the reception didn't

budge as she shoved against it with her bottom and simultaneously tried to secure her wayward hair in a rubber band.

'Ouch,' she muttered just as it gave way, and two firm hands grasped her shoulders. The hands spun her around firmly. She looked up. A long way up. The muscular frame of her impatient visitor blocked the doorway.

'Tiffany-Jane Stevens?' His voice reverberated through her, deep and rumbling. Not unlike thunder — which matched the expression on his face.

She shivered. 'Yes?'

'Scott Devin. Tie your damn shoes, take off that ridiculous skirt, and meet me in my office.' He spun around and stalked off.

Shit! TJ stared at his departing back with a sinking feeling in her stomach. Scott Devin. Her new boss. He was a week early. It was definitely going to be a bad day.

Scott slammed the door to his predecessor's office. As if he didn't have enough on his plate already, he'd arrived at his newly acquired dealership at 7.30am to find the place locked up, no staff, and customers queuing at the door. If it wasn't for the set of keys the agent had given him at handover, they'd all still be out on the driveway awaiting the arrival of his leading hand.

He hated to be kept waiting, especially when he had so much to do. Irritation ripped through him. She hadn't even recognised him as her new boss because she'd been so focused on using his staff to tow her own car. And to set him aside like that ... What if he'd been a customer? No wonder Mal's Motors was in trouble. Which was just one of the reasons he was here. Voted Most Successful Businessman of the Year, he'd acquired several struggling car dealerships nationwide and turned them into multi-million-dollar enterprises.

He picked up the latest edition of *Professional Spotlight* then tossed it aside again with a grunt. His face stared back at him from the cover, silent and brooding. Here he was in the foothills of Perth with his latest acquisition, but, instead of feeling the usual drive to turn it around, he felt unsettled.

Somewhere in the rat race on the east coast, he'd lost his passion for doing what he did. And the reason for that still posed a threat, even as far away as across the country. He stared out the window at the hills in the distance. If only he could make the last twelve months go away.

He'd thought he'd find a new challenge in a dealership that had once been a country workshop. Now it was surrounded by a growing suburb on the main highway into Perth. Favoured by the locals, it maintained its country atmosphere, with all the facilities of a small town. The potential for growth was huge and the challenge was certainly there. Would it be enough to start over?

A firm tap on his door heralded the arrival of Tiffany-Jane Stevens. He shook his head and squared his shoulders. He'd not expected TJ Stevens to be a pint-sized, stiletto-wearing cannon ball in a mini skirt who arrived late to work, left customers out in the cold and her employees unsupervised.

'Come in.'

TJ opened the door and strode up to his desk, hands firmly on her hips. 'Mr Devin, I'm sorry I was late and not here to greet you, but I have a huge workload today, so can we hurry this up? I'm happy to set a meeting with you after closing time.'

She'd tied her boots and taken off the skirt. Her hi-vis work jacket remained unzipped, *Here Comes Trouble* printed in black on the grey T-shirt she wore underneath it. Scott pulled out his chair and sat down. Her T-shirt said it all.

'No kidding,' he muttered.

'I beg your pardon?' TJ looked at him uncertainly.

'Sit down, TJ.'

'I'd rather stand if that's okay with you?' Green eyes clashed with his. 'I'm running a bit behind.'

He stood up again. 'Punctuality is important in a

leading hand. You're meant to be setting an example for your team.'

She narrowed her gaze on his face. 'My car broke down. It's not like I overslept.'

Scott acknowledged the tinge of sarcasm behind her words, but he pushed on. 'Your car broke down. Did you think to ring someone and let them know?'

TJ shook her head. 'My phone battery is running low. I need to put it on charge.'

'Perhaps you should have thought of that before you left a nightclub to come straight to work. You were an hour late!' How else could she explain the mini skirt and stilettos at 8.30 in the morning?

'Is that where you think I've come from?' Her back stiffened, drawing her to her full height of just over five foot. She sucked in her bottom lip and chewed on it, clearly biting back an angry response. 'You know what? You're right, of course. I'm sorry. It won't happen again.'

'Damn straight, it won't happen again. You also broke a few safety rules.' He ticked them off on his fingers. 'You didn't secure your shoe laces before entering the workspace, presenting a trip hazard. You wore a frilly skirt over your protective wear, presenting a snarl hazard, and you traipsed across a greasy floor in open-toed, *stiletto heels*!' His irritation escalated as he counted off her sins.

Scott watched her face pale as the implications

dawned. She was the team leader, the one to set the example. Breaking safety rules could mean only one thing. 'You're fired.' He delivered the final blow and sat back down. 'Pack up your things. I'll have HR make up your severance package.' He tried not to feel like an arsehole as she quietly turned and left the office.

'Egotistical, pompous, east coast *arse*!' Seething, TJ marched back into the workshop. She hated it when people made assumptions. 'Meeting, boys.' She waved the team over to the clocking machine. They downed their tools and gathered around her. 'That was your new boss. I've been fired.' She held up a hand to stem the grumbled responses. 'No, he's right. I broke the rules. When Tony gets back, he'll take over as team leader until Mr Devin finds a replacement for me. I expect you all to respect his wishes and work with him.'

'But, TJ, what about our contracts?' Terry tipped back his cap to rub at his shaved head. 'We don't want to work with anyone else.'

TJ's heart hitched. She'd worked so hard to get Terry off meth. Two years later, he was on the straight and narrow, enrolled in a mature-aged apprenticeship, and mentoring the younger kids.

'I'll still be around. Just not here. No setbacks, guys. We've worked too hard to let the program slide. It's all up to you now.' She stopped as she saw their eyes shift to the observation window where customers could watch the work being carried out from the safety of the reception area.

Scott Devin stood watching. Probably making sure she left the premises without stealing anything. The sour thought ran through her mind even as her skin tingled from the force of his gaze boring into her back. She stiffened her spine. TJ snapped her fingers in the air and drew her team's attention back to her. 'Guys! Tony will need your support.'

They nodded their agreement, just as Tony strode into the shop. 'What's going on?'

'You're in charge.'

Terry pushed his cap back on. 'That new arsehole just fired her.'

'What? Why?' Tony looked up to where Scott stood behind the glass.

He made to push past TJ toward the reception, but she held him back. 'Let it go, mate.'

'But TJ, he has no idea —'

'Let it go. He'll find out soon enough. I'll have to leave Sheila here overnight. I'll arrange for a tow truck in the morning. Back to work now, guys.' She waved them away.

Tony stood his ground. 'It's not fair.'

'It's the rules. How bad is Sheila?'

Tony shook his head. 'Hard to say. She smelled a

little burnt. We'll have to take the cylinder head off for pressure testing. Lucky you know not to push her too far when she starts overheating. Hopefully the damage will be minimal.' He indicated with a thumb over his shoulder to the driveway. 'Marty's just getting her settled.'

She hooked an arm through Tony's and steered him out the workshop onto the drive. Out the corner of her eye, she saw Scott Devin on the move too. As heart-stoppingly gorgeous in person as he was in the magazine, he towered at least a foot or more over her, built like a brick wall. The tailored business suit enhanced rather than hid the strong, muscular body underneath. Chiselled features tapered into a round jaw darkened by stubble, a slightly crooked nose and dark blue eyes that could stop a freight train in its tracks with just one look. Jet black hair cut neat and short … It didn't matter how attractive he was, he was still a pompous arse.

They stepped out onto the driveway where Sheila sat, offering an occasional hiss and spit. Steam still floated through the radiator grille. The 1975 Holden Gemini SL Sedan was a patchwork of faded red and body filler grey. Clear lacquer blistered in the areas that had not been filled. Once restoration was complete, she would be a collector's item for enthusiasts. For TJ, even worthless, it was one of her most valued possessions.

'*This* is your car?' Scott stepped up next to her.

She looked up at him, desperately wanting to wipe the smirk off his face. Instead, she moved to lift the bonnet. 'Marty, hit the release cable.' She pulled her heat resistant gloves out of her pocket and put them on.

'Now she remembers the safety rules,' Scott muttered.

TJ stiffened until she thought her spine would snap but ignored him. She had nothing more to lose. Only good manners made her bite down on a response. There was no reason to give him the satisfaction. She lifted the bonnet and secured it with the metal stay. Bracing her hands on the front of the car, she leaned in to look for broken fan belts or a damaged fan blade. None. That was good.

'No blown hoses, TJ.' Tony snapped off his torch. 'Radiator's leaking through the core. Probably warped the cylinder head a little.'

'Let's hope it's only a little.' TJ stepped back and straightened. She felt Scott's muscular warmth at her back where he'd been peering over her shoulder.

'As riveting as this is, can we all get back to work now? We're running a little behind schedule.'

She swallowed the sarcasm she wanted to respond with. TJ turned to face him. 'Yes. I'll get her picked up in the morning if it's okay for her to stay overnight?'

He shrugged. 'Do I have a choice?'

'Yes, you can say no.' She pulled off her gloves and shoved them into his chest, leaving him no option but to close his hands around them. Her patience was running out fast. TJ pushed past him. 'Marty, have you still got my keys?'

'Yep, why?'

'Toolbox key is the third one in. Go inside and pack up my tools, please.'

'Say what, TJ?' Marty stopped dead in the middle of dropping Sheila's bonnet back into place.

'I don't work here anymore. Tony, can you please drop off my toolbox on your way home tonight?' TJ patted Marty on the back. 'Tony will take care of you, Marty.'

'Sure, TJ, but —' The terror on the boy's face made her heart ache. She was the one who picked him up every time he got sucked back into back-alley business.

She dropped her hand onto his shoulder. 'It's okay, Marty. You've got my number. Call me whenever you need to.'

Marty dropped the bonnet a little harder than necessary and stormed off into the shop, his shoulders rigid as he swore under his breath.

'That'll be 20c in the swear jar, mate. Tony, you've got this, right?'

Tony shot Scott Devin a look of pure contempt before answering. 'Sure, TJ. Drop off the toolbox, take care of Marty and Sheila.'

'Back to work then. You've got a shop to run.'

He aimed another killer look at the new boss before he complied.

TJ pulled her mobile phone out of her pocket and dialled.

Silence hung heavily as she waited for an answer. She couldn't resist a look at Scott. He held her gaze until she looked away.

'Rob, I need a lift home. Yes, now. I'll explain when you get here.' She pressed the screen to end the call. 'I'll just get dressed and then I'll get out of your hair.'

'You do that, Tiger,' he answered as she walked away.

Tagged (Book2 – Unfinished Business) can be purchased from your favourite bookseller. If they don't have it, ask them or your local library to order it in for you.

Dear Reader.

This book has been written and edited using Australian / UK English grammar and punctuation conventions because the story is set in Australia. For more information on the differences between UK and US language and punctuation, please consider reading this article: https://tinyurl.com/56tkbh6a

If you enjoyed this book, please consider leaving a review on BookBub, Goodreads or the platform you purchased it from. If you would prefer to email me, please visit the contact page on my website at https://juanitakees.com/contact/. I do love to hear from readers and welcome your feedback.

Kind regards

Juanita Kees

Other Books by Juanita Kees

JUANITA KEES
THE GODS OF OAKLEIGH